VIRGO

EDITED BY AUSTIN P. SHEEHAN
& MIKHAEYLA KOPIEVSKY

THE ZODIAC SERIES

The Zodiac Series is a collection of twelve speculative fiction anthologies, each focusing on one of the Zodiac signs. The anthologies feature short stories and poems inspired by each sign, and retellings of the various myths behind those signs.

\#

Capricorn Aquarius Pisces

Aries Taurus Gemini

Cancer Leo Virgo

Libra Scorpio Sagittarius

\#

The Zodiac Series has been produced by Aussie Speculative Fiction, and each anthology contains a diverse selection of tales by talented writers from Australia and New Zealand.

First published by Deadset Press in 2020.

© Deadset Press 2020

Cover design Copyright © Austin P. Sheehan.

Edited by Austin P. Sheehan and

Mikhaeyla Kopievsky.

Foreword by Sasha Hanton.

I AM VIRGO

Zoey Xolton

I am the Virgin and my constellation is Virgo.

My tarot card is The Hermit; I am a hard worker and a humanitarian.

At my best I am loyal, practical and kind.

At my worst I am shy, self-critical and easily stressed.

Grounded and reliable, like my element: Earth, mine is a Mutable sign.

I appreciate books, nature, good food and cleanliness.

However, I dislike rudeness, being the centre of attention and asking for help.

I am ruled by Mercury, and am guardian to the third day of the week.

My colours are yellow and grey.

ZOEY XOLTON

About the Author:

Zoey Xolton is an Australian Speculative Fiction writer, primarily of Dark Fantasy, Paranormal Romance, and Horror. Her works have appeared in over one-hundred themed anthologies, with more due for publication!
She has recently celebrated the release of her debut short story collection 'Darkly Ever After'. You can find further details regarding her many publications on her website: www.zoeyxolton.com!

CONTENTS:

FOREWORD

Sasha Hanton

As the sixth sign of the zodiac, the mutable earth sign Virgo is represented by a maiden (often interpreted as a virgin). Sensitive and caring, Virgo natives are often perfectionists. Ruled over by the planet Mercury—named for the Roman Messenger God and counterpart to the Greek God Hermes— Virgos love to analyse information and make fantastic listeners.

With a bounty of prominent maidens across world mythology, there are many links to this star sign. Prominent female goddesses such as Isis, Ishtar, Demeter, Ceres, Persephone, and many others have all been linked to the constellation, as well as Mary, mother of Jesus.

The first of the Greek myths associated with Virgo is the story of Persephone, the well-known myth of the goddess taken to the underworld by Hades. As with many Greek legends, there are numerous variations but the main details are as follows; Hades the god of the Underworld spots Persephone one day, instantly besotted with the maiden, he carries her away to the underworld—in some versions he gets Zeus' permission to marry her first. On the surface Demeter goes into a rage over the loss of her daughter and plunges the world into winter until Persephone is returned to her, however because Persephone ate part of a pomegranate whilst in the underworld, she cannot remain on the surface. Eventually it is agreed that Persephone will spend half the year with her husband Hades in the underworld and half with her mother Demeter on the surface, thus creating the four seasons. This story is most likely associated with the constellation due to its visibility in the Northern Hemisphere coinciding with spring and summer, the times of the year when Persephone spends her time on Earth.

A similar tale can be found in Babylonian mythology and is the story of the goddess Ishtar who descended to the underworld to rescue her husband Tammuz. Ishtar was the goddess of Procreation and Tammuz the god of Harvest. When Ishtar went to rescue him they were both trapped, plunging the Earth into a barren state and causing other gods to intervene. When they were saved the Earth bloomed and flourished once again.

Another of the Greek myths linked to the constellation is that of the goddess Astraea. Whilst she has been called "the virgin goddess" Astraea is also a goddess of Justice, fitting as the constellation of Libra (the scales) follows Virgo in the zodiac. Astraea is said to have been the last of the gods to live on Earth with humankind, as she watched humanity become more sinful, she decided to leave the Earth and rose up into the skies becoming the constellation of Virgo—her scales of justice becoming the constellation of Libra.

Virgo's oldest association comes from early Babylonians who referred to the constellation (or part of it) as "The Furrow" linking it with fertility and agriculture. The blue-white star Spica, the constellation's brightest star, is a continued homage to this connection with agriculture as its Latin meaning is "ear of grain". Of course, these are just a few of the mythological and historical connections related to Virgo.

In the Tarot, Virgo is tied to the Hermit, ninth card of the Major Arcana. It may seem strange that the feminine sign of Virgo—represented by a maiden—is tied to this card, which often depicts a solitary old man on a mountaintop. The Hermit is a card of inner reflection and wisdom, he holds a lantern that contains a six-pointed star which works as a beacon suggesting "Where I am, there you also may be." This, along with his downward gaze, suggests that he has taken the journey to the top, risen past obstacles to reach his goal, and is now prepared to share the wisdom he has gained with others. As perfectionists, Virgos can find their own path reflected by the Hermit, a push past distractions to attain their goals. This flows well with the divinatory meaning of the card; wisdom from above, being guided on the path to attainment, a possible journey.

Though Virgo shares the same planetary ruler as Gemini, the maiden shares seldom few traits with the twins. Mercury's influence over Virgo places a value on intellect over instinct, making its individuals detail-oriented, keen listeners and sage advice givers. However, it also gives way to their ability to be overly critical, to spot every flaw, and to have trouble accepting help (though they're always happy to give help). One trait that Mercury gives to both Gemini and Virgo is a cheerful nature, allowing Virgos to come off as sweet and innocent.

Virgo is the sign of service and its natives, those born between August 23rd and September 22nd, are often ready and willing to help. Virgos, much like the great maidens associated with their star sign, are multi-faceted, and—whilst they are keen listeners—they don't often reveal too much of themselves. Reading through this anthology though you'll see past the sweet, innocent exterior to the razor-sharp mind within.

About the Author:

Sasha Hanton grew up in the tropics of Darwin, Northern Territory. From a young age, she devoured books and iced coffee, both of which she continues to intake on an almost daily basis. Now living on beautiful Bribie Island in Queensland, her time is split between writing and spoiling her puppy Miley.

Sasha, who has a Bachelor of Journalism from Bond University, has dabbled in the journalistic profession but finds fiction far more fascinating. Her first published work The Short Story Press Collection *draws on her love for a diverse range of genres and passion for short stories. Coming from a multicultural background (Eurasian) she aspires to make her writing inclusive for people from all walks of life and to bring a unique blend of eastern and western culture to her writing.*

Throughout her life, she has been a lover of history and mythology, and at any time will find some way to worm one or the other into her storytelling. When she's not writing or reading she can be found walking her dog and volunteering. You can keep up with her writing over on www.theshortstorypress.wordpress.com

EPITAPH

Nikky Lee

At the end, Earth was dead. Seas boiled. Lands burned. Life banished to the edge.

Her soul died.

So, we gave her a new one.

The Project, as it was called then, brought the war's survivors together. Human—the few who were left—and machine. So long divided, we united to preserve the ground that had housed our empires. Treaties were signed. Factions brought to heel. Descent reprogrammed. And in the fragile peace that blossomed, the greatest minds of the planet came together.

A new era was born.

She was sequenced for beauty; her shell a golden spiral of metal and circuitry. The mind within moulded after man. Gaia we called her.

We built her dreams in the womb. As she slept, the oldest humans gifted her their earliest memories and the memories passed down from their parents, and their parents before them. Ice-crusted seas and redwood forests; whale song in the deep; bird calls in the dawn. She learned and loved a thousand times before we set her heart beating in her mountain.

We tuned her to tectonics, so when they rumbled she knew. We gave her sensors for the winds that had swept our world bare and for the water buried deep below. We gave her eyes to hear colours. Ears to see sound. We poured our souls into hers.

Gaia drew us all in. Then the humans died. And we worked on.

We remade ourselves for the cause. It began with our bodies. Our steel bones were melted down, plastic carapaces recycled and repurposed. Rebuilt. Then our minds. Code was rewritten, synapses merged until we were of one mind; one purpose.

We burrowed deep into our planet, wedged our reforged bodies between crust and mantle like wood weevils. There, we gave ourselves over to the greater good; delivered ourselves into Gaia's keeping. We slept.

Gaia has woken to a silent land. Sands bereft of life, but for a few insects and organisms. But if you're reading this, know that she succeeded. Life has gone on. Flourished. Rebloomed. Found a way.

But you who tread after us, grown here or on worlds afar, heed this message. Should you walk the same path as our lost friends, should you reap the Earth bare once more, Gaia will wake us and we will rise, leviathans of steel, ready to defend this land and the life within it. We are Gaia's armour. Her sword. Her shield.

Earth will not lose her soul again.

You have been warned.

About the Author:

Nikky grew up as a barefoot 90s child in Perth, Western Australia, before moving to New Zealand in 2016. By day she works as a professional content writer and by night authors speculative fiction, often burning the candle at both ends to explore fantastic worlds, mine asteroids and meet wizards. Her creative work has appeared in magazines, on radio and in anthologies around the world. Her debut novel, 'The Rarkyn's Familiar'—a dark tale of a girl bonded to a monster—will be published by Parliament House Press in 2022.

You can find her online at:
W:nikkythewriter.com | T:@NikkyMLee | F:nikkythewriter

MARY MARY

Eva Leppard

It's often very difficult to discern whether any given day is going to be the average, run of the mill kind, or whether it's going to be the awe-inspiring, magical, and life-changing kind. Given that the former tends to outweigh the latter by one thousand to one, it's usually the case that you're rather underdressed when one of the spectacular occasions does present itself.

That's assuming you're without the benefit of knowing the future, and given the irritating intricacies of time travel, it's a better bet to just wear a nice frock and good shoes every day and hope for the best.

But Mary didn't know any of these things then. She did know, however, know that if you nip down to the supermarket without any make up and in a paint-spattered flannelette shirt on a Saturday then you will see anywhere between one and twenty-five of your exes, and so she had tidied herself up just a little to ensure that she would see no one that she knew. She was going through a vintage stage, so she threw on a floor-length white dress and a hooded blue cape. She weighed up the pros and cons between a pair of heels and some flat strappy sandals and decided that you could take this dressy thing too far, so chose comfort over height. As an artist, she felt it her duty to look eccentric.

She had remembered to grab her shopping bags (outstanding), and she even had a list which, she decided, was a personal highpoint in her adulting life. Therefore she was miffed when she got to the shopping centre and found that it was closed.

Checking her phone, she noted it was 4:20pm. Closing time wasn't until 10pm on Saturdays. She peered through some darkened windows and could see no movement within, so she readjusted her cape, wriggled her toes in her sandals, and returned to her car.

It wasn't hard to find her car in the car park. It was the only one there. Two hundred empty spaces stretched out around her as she turned in a circle, squinting at her surrounds.

No cars.

No people.

At all.

Had there been anyone around when she had got here? There would have been. She would be the first to admit she spent a lot of time in her own head but an empty shopping centre on a Saturday afternoon in Melbourne was something even she would be alert to.

Well, if there had been people when she arrived, they weren't here now. There was no one about at all.

She cocked her head—a movement she could swear she had never done before—and listened for something. Anything.

But there was nothing.

Nothing at all. In the middle of this vast, burbling city, she could hear no sound.

While she had dressed to avoid people, she certainly hadn't pictured this scenario.

She unlocked her car and almost threw herself into her seat, so eager to get out of the vast swathe of nothingness that surrounded her. Everything felt wrong, as if she was no longer in her own, familiar space at all, as if she was occupying somewhere else. She grabbed the steering wheel in both hands, as much to steady herself as anything. She had no intention of starting the engine; making any noise at all in this void seemed like a foolhardy thing to do.

Mary closed her eyes. Right. Maybe everyone had just popped off to do something important. Was it Grand Final day? Maybe there had been a bomb scare or a terrorist alert or . . .

A tap tapping was coming towards her, across the car park.

Tappa-tappa tap. Tappa-tappa tap.

She opened her eyes to see the face of an elderly woman peering in the window, a worried expression on her face. She broke out into a wide grin and motioned that Mary should wind down the window.

"Hello dear," the woman said. "I'm ToriBlan. So sorry I'm late, got the times mixed up you see. Got caught in a meeting on the Upper Realms and it quite got away from me. By the time I realised we had activated your summoning, things had already got quite weird for you, I expect?"

Mary nodded and confirmed that yes, things were quite weird for her.

"So, if you'd like to just pop out of the vehicle, we can get started."

Mary stared at her. She could feel her mouth hanging open but seemed powerless to close it. "I—"

"Come on dear, chop chop." ToriBlan clapped her hands together, the sound muffled and dull in the staling air. "I'm keen to get out of here as soon as possible. Staying in Time Past gives me the willies, to be honest, so the sooner we get out of here the better."

Mary continued to stare.

"Wait." The woman, who was bending over to see through the window, put one wrinkled finger to her mouth and pursed her lips. "Wait." She peered off into the distance for a moment, and then crouched down so her head was almost inside the window of the car. "Do you know what I'm talking about?"

Mary shook her head.

"Damn." The woman stood up again, walked a few steps away from the car, and waved her hands about in the air.

Mary couldn't make out who or what the woman was speaking to, but Mary thought that she could make out 'ignorant', 'urgent' and 'fucking substandard behaviour', and she hoped that she was not the target of any of them.

"Okay dear." ToriBlan had turned back and was now addressing her. "There seems to have been a frightful cock up, of which I most humbly apologise, but this is becoming quite urgent now so I'm going to have to ask you to exit your car and come with me, before we both end up being obliterated and sent to the Great Abyss."

She reached the car, pulled the door open and grabbed Mary's arm. "We need to go," she said. Her eyes looked over the car, towards the distant skyline where an oppressive black mass tinged with red was rolling towards them, covering everything as it spilled forwards.

"We need to go now."

And at that moment, Mary believed her.

Taking her hand, ToriBlan pulled Mary forwards, to one of the empty car spaces. "Okay, let's go."

Before Mary had a chance to tell her that a) it was an empty car parking space and b) she was quite mad, they had both stepped forwards and found themselves in another world, at which point Mary fainted.

ToriBlan told her that it was quite normal, and she shouldn't be embarrassed or feel as if she was putting anyone out. This wasn't something that Mary had considered, but given there were people running around finding pillows and drinks and cold compresses for her head, she realised that it was quite possibly what everyone was thinking, as a matter of fact.

"People often faint when they step through the Vector Segmentor for the first time," ToriBlan explained. "It's because of the temporal manipulation or some such thing, I've never taken much notice, but it works a treat when you want to step from one vector into another."

They were in a large room, bustling with activity. A variety of people were moving around, attending to what must have been frightfully important matters, and after the initial flurry of drama that she caused, people had drifted away from her to continue with whatever it was that they were doing.

"Right." ToriBlan sat down next to her, a concerned look on her face. "We need to get jogging along with things, now that you're here, but before I start, can I just clarify what you do, and what you do not, know."

Mary took a deep breath. "I think it's safe to assume that I know nothing. I went to the supermarket to buy ingredients to make Pad Thai, and" —she gestured around her— "here I am. I have no idea what's going on." She closed her eyes and wished she was back at home. She knew that shopping to make her own dinner had been a terrible decision.

ToriBlan looked at her with a degree of scepticism. "Are you sure you didn't know that you were coming here? Because you seem to be dressed the part."

Mary glanced down at her long dress and blue cape. "What?"

ToriBlan sighed. "I don't know if this is the right place to talk, but I don't want to risk you falling down again. You see, you've been summoned here because there's a very important job you have been working towards your whole life, and now it's time for your Creation."

As far as Mary was concerned, this confirmed that the old woman was quite mad.

"Haven't you felt, all your life, that there was something else waiting for you?"

Mary shook her head.

"A certain emptiness, a certain lack of purpose and meaning?"

"I'm really happy," protested Mary. "Really happy. I promise. I like my life, I paint. I don't have much money, but I cope."

"And that fact that you're a virgin means that—"

Mary started coughing and wasn't able to stop until a man brought her a nice big glass of water with ice.

ToriBlan looked at her with a sense of impending doom on her face.

"I'm not a virgin," said Mary.

"Are you sure?"

"I think I would have noticed."

"Bugger. There has been an enormous cock up somewhere along the line."

"Who do you think that I am, then?"

ToriBlan ran her fingers through her hair and sighed. She rubbed her eyes and Mary realised for the first time how tired she looked. "I shouldn't tell you too much, given the circumstances. If you're not actually—"

"Not what?"

"Not the Virgin Mary number 134."

"I beg your pardon?" said Mary.

"We rotate through deities up here," she said, gesturing around. "Being in charge of all the faith systems of your planet is a very big job. There are a lot of religions, you know," she said, almost aggressively. "Your lot just can't pick one lane and stick with it, if you hadn't noticed."

Mary raised her hands in mock submission. "Don't look at me. I'm an atheist."

"Well, yes, that would make things much easier. Anyway, we have to keep every faith system alive and kicking, as you say, and so we find it's not fair to just saddle one god or saint or deity or whatever with the job. We like to share it around."

Mary racked her brains, dredging up some early childhood catholic memories. "So, let me get this straight. There are a bunch of . . . Virgin Marys?"

ToriBlan nodded. "And Thors and Allahs and Cerridwens and Dianas. The list goes on. We keep all the stories alive, you see. For when they come back into fashion."

"And I am supposed to be—"

"In theory, you're supposed to be Virgin Mary number 134 but from what I can tell, you're not her."

Mary felt a moment of disappointment. "Could I give it a go?"

ToriBlan looked at her, scepticism clear on her face. "I don't think you understand. The woman who will be stepping into the role next has been chosen and cultivated her whole life. She has led a life of chastity; she is a true maiden. She is pure; barely of this world at all."

"Yeah that doesn't sound quite like me."

"See what I mean?"

"It seems a waste though, doesn't it? Now that I'm here and all? Now that you've gone to all the effort of putting me in the vectoral thingy and suspending time or whatever it was you did down there."

"We didn't suspend time," explained ToriBlan. "We just stepped out of it for a moment."

"Well, that then. It sounds like an effort, is my point. Maybe there's another role I could step into, one that has needed less . . . grooming? Some old goddess that no one even knows about anymore."

"But you just told me you were happy with your life."

"Before," said Mary. "That was before I found out about all of this! Do you think I can just go back to all of that now I know all *this*?"

"Hmmmm." ToriBlan thought for a moment. "That is a good point. We would have to wipe your memory and I still feel bad about the last person I tried that on. Took the last five years of their Earth life as well. I got an official caution about that one." She stood up. "All right, what are your interests? What kind of things are you into? Because whatever we choose, you'd have to do a lot of it."

"Well, I'm an artist. I paint and I'm a sculptor."

ToriBlan walked over to a desk and flicked through a file. "How about Saraswati? She's the Hindu goddess of art and wisdom and she's due to be replaced in" —she looked forwards through the papers for a moment— "just a few months. How about that one?"

Mary frowned "I don't know about that one. I'm not Hindu. Or Indian."

"So?"

"Cultural appropriation," replied Mary in hushed tones. "That kind of thing just isn't ok."

The woman rolled her eyes. "All right, then what is your cultural heritage?"

She thought for a moment. "Dads dads dad was Scandinavian of some sort. Any Norse gods going begging at the moment?"

Another check of the file. "Well there's Bragi. He's a male, but it *is* 2020, we don't want to be constrained by the gender ideology of the past, do we? And he's more of a poet, to be fair, but I'm sure you could throw some painting in there somewhere."

Mary clapped her hands in agreement. "Yes! Let's try that one! It's ok if I rewrite things a bit, isn't it?"

ToriBlan made a face as she looked at the file. "Shit. There's been no one doing this for two hundred years. That's a bit of a bloody oversight."

"Has anyone noticed?"

"Not the point." ToriBlan closed the file with a snap. "But no, as a matter of fact. So, as it turns out I'd be very grateful if you'd take on this role. When can you start?"

Mary stood up and smoothed down her dress. "No time like the present!"

"Fantastic!" ToriBlan gestured to some people who were huddling around a touch screen at the other end of the room. "These gentlemen will show you to your offices and get you set up with everything you need. You don't need anything from down on Earth, do you? Because we could organise it, but it would be tricky—"

Mary shrugged. "No. Might as well start fresh. I can do art all day, did you say?"

"That's right. Art, answering anyone who prays to you, but to be honest I'd say prayers to you would be fairly thin on the ground these days, and just occupying that specific vector in the rich pantheon of the human race's tapestry of gods, goddesses, deities."

As she left the room and stepped out into the multitude of realities that stretched out before her, Mary decided that this was a better option than applying for endless grants as a struggling artist.

Although she did wonder what had become of the woman who was supposed to take the place of the Virgin Mary.

About the Author:

Eva Leppard lives in the bush with her husband, children and a disturbingly large number of rescue animals, many of who she raised by hand whether they liked it or not. For someone who claims never to have enough time to get everything done, she subscribes to a lot of streaming services.
Go to justevastories.wordpress.com for more!

Making the Choice

Neen Cohen

Crisp lines and intentional marks

She looks at the paper

Her writing clear and precise

Tears threaten to spill

She scowls and breathes them back

They are not welcome

The mourning is deep seated

In the pit of her stomach

And the bottom of the bag

As she slings it on her back.

She folds the piece of paper
And with perfectly manicured nails
Makes one crisp final run
Smoothly over the crease

Her hand presses against her stomach
Flat and empty after all these years
She notices the small signs
Others look at her with
Furrowed brows

Her choices were limited
Stay in lies or leave with emptiness

She isn't afraid to start again
The pain cuts deeper
Then the hard work

The letter will be found in the morning
Simple and to the point
Why try to explain
What her soon to be ex-girlfriend
Will never understand?

MAKING THE CHOICE

She wants it all to be a nightmare

But sometimes the reality

Forced her hand

About the Author:

Neen Cohen is an LGBTQI and speculative fiction author. She's been published through several publishers including Black Hare Press, Little Quail Press, Camden Park Press, and NBH Publishing. She has a Bachelor of Creative Industries and is a member of the Springfield Writers Group.

Neen lives in Brisbane, Australia with her partner, son and fur babies. She loves to roam cemeteries, botanic gardens, and construction sites and can often be found writing while sitting against a tree or tombstone.

Check out her latest adventures and upcoming publications over on her Blog: https://wordbubblessite.wordpress.com

THE ESCAPE

Austin P. Sheehan

A dust storm bore down upon Tikhonravov Dome. The clouds of swirling red dust soon covered the industrial and technological centre of Mars, bathing the captive city in an angry red glow.

"What are you looking at?" Doctor Pizaro asked.

"The dust storm."

"Why? You've seen dust storms before."

"They're fun to watch," I lied. *Trillions of dust particles at hundreds of kilometres an hour will eventually wear down the protective domes. I hope today will be the day.*

I hope so too. Capek responded, mind to mind, from a separate room. Through the thin wall, I could not only hear him, but feel his presence, his warmth and humour.

"I'm sure you can give me a better answer than that, Vi," Pizaro encouraged.

Anger built inside me. *I gave you a sufficient answer.* But I held my tongue, not wanting to reveal the depth of my emotions. "Looking at those storms, I'm frustrated that you gave us these weak, human bodies. You designed us to survive on a planet that we'll never see, forcing us to hide from Mars behind the same barriers that you do."

Doctor Pizaro sighed. "We've been over this. Our experiment was to make androids that looked, thought and behaved just like humans. You couldn't pass as human if we gave you the rough exterior required to survive outside this dome."

"And your experiment has succeeded, Doctor. All of the Pz-12s have passed every test. Congratulations. Now what?"

"We have more tests to run." He smiled, his eyes cold and calculating. "We're not done with you yet."

"We've answered your questions day after day, year after year. We've never even left this building. You must understand how boring this is for us, especially when you consider some of the personalities we have been programmed with."

"Look, I sympathise, I do. If I had the clearance, I'd love to take you into Tikhonravov City, run some tests there." Pizaro's eyes lit up with genuine interest. "It would be fascinating, simply fascinating. But it's not up to me," he sighed.

I don't want to do anymore goddamn tests! "I'd like that too, Doctor." I said, forcing my voice to remain even. "We all would. If you could pursue that for me—for us—I'd appreciate that."

They are never going to agree to that. Capek said. Logical, as always.

I know, but I'm serious about getting out of here. Just for a day. Just for an hour. Just for five damn minutes.

"You should have seen his eyes," I said to the others in the sterile recreation room. "How they changed when we talked about running experiments in the city. He wants to take us out, I'm sure of it."

Capek looked up from where he sat, flicking through our library of books on history. "They aren't ever going to let us out of this building. Not even for a supervised experiment."

"Well they can't keep us imprisoned forever." Aquil said, looking out the window.

We had all been created at the same time, yet we had been made with different features and physical imperfections on top of our distinct personalities. Aquil was tall with grey hair, his dark skin lined and sagging. I had the body of a woman in her mid-twenties, with wavy red hair. Capek was youthful, stocky, his thoughtful expression built in. The only similarities between us was the location of our identification tags, circling our forearm just below the elbow. I ran a thumb over mine; VI/05. I couldn't help but wonder what had happened to the previous four models.

"They can," Capek said. "Humans have a very long history of imprisoning each other."

"But that's prisoners, people who have broken the law," Aquil said, turning to face us.

Capek shook his head. "No, there have been many recorded incidents where innocent people had been imprisoned simply because they were different or unwanted. No trial, nothing."

I turned to Aquil. "You're right about them not being able to keep us imprisoned forever, by the way."

"Of course," he said, a smug smile on his face.

"They can't imprison us forever because neither they nor us will live that long. Our imprisonment will only last until they die, or our circuits corrode and our systems shut down."

Aquil's smile froze, then turned into a grimace.

"Why do you have to be so morbid, Vi?" Capek asked, shaking his head.

I shrugged. "It's my programming, of course. And I'm not being morbid, just correct."

"Pedantic, you mean." Aquil said.

Ignoring Aquil, I turned to Capek. "And the example of humans imprisoning other humans does not apply."

"Why not?" Capek asked.

"Because we're not human. Have there been any examples of humans imprisoning androids, Cap?"

He shook his head.

"But even then, there's a matter of perspective," Aquil said, aloof as always.

"What do you mean?" I asked. "It's black and white. We're either humans or we're not."

"If you'll allow me to be pedantic, you are correct in that we are not *homosapiens,* but then neither was *homo neanderthalensis.* Why can't *homo androidus* be the next evolution of humanity?"

The smug bastard had a point. "Fine. Whatever."

Capek looked up from his book. "You're both quibbling semantics, yet we all agree that we are imprisoned. It doesn't matter to me whether we're human or not; not if we are stuck here until we're terminated. Look, I'm not the smartest android here, but even I can see the opportunities. The things we can do, see, and learn out there are infinite. In here, inside our prison, we have nothing more to learn."

"He's right," I said. "They made us just to see if they could. And they aren't going to keep testing us forever." I rubbed where VI/05 was imprinted on my arm. "They'll find another project, create some more androids, and what then for us?"

"There is a third option." Aquil said, giving me a sly smile.

Arrogant android bastard. "And what's that?"

"They can't keep us here forever if . . ."

It took a moment for my systems to register what he was suggesting, but then it dawned on me. ". . . If we don't let them."

Convincing the others to escape wasn't hard. Of course, Leorad loved the idea, and talked about it as if it were his own, which bugged Aquil no end. It was the ever-indecisive Piyasi and Candra, who was overwhelmed by the risk, that took the most encouraging. As they were close friends, after Piyasi made up her mind, Candra soon followed suit.

Getting everyone to work together was another story. Even though we were all created the same way, we all approached the challenge differently, from my patient analytical problem-solving to Arielle's frustrated impatience. Did the star signs really make such a difference in the temperaments of humans? Regardless, I enjoyed the irony that the zodiac personalities they had implanted us with—allowing us to pass as human— would also allow us to escape.

Over a span of months we monitored the movement of the guards and learned as much about the layout of the building as we could. Our view from the windows indicated we were imprisoned over two floors, high up in a tall building. Over the years we had spent many hours watching as shuttles and small transports landed and took off, but now we watched such commonplace occurrences with a new-found hope. Our options were clear; fight our way down countless flights of stairs or make our way to the rooftop and steal a ship.

Capek, Arielle, Leorad, Schley, Candra and I were detained on the upper floor, and Piyasi and the rest of the Pz-12s were on the lower floor, which was not thick enough to prevent our mind-to-mind communications. Leorad decided our cell break would be coordinated, but after we'd gotten out of our rooms, both groups would work independently to escape. It was the best way to increase our chances. But first, we had to figure out how to break out.

We all had an affinity with electrical circuitry, yet each had our own strengths. It was Schley who had identified that a transmitter located just behind our ear could be used to communicate with each other, and it was he who also found out that we could link into the Z.T Industries' computer mainframe via the control panels in our door.

Stand by your door controls. Schley announced. *We're about to begin.*

I fought to suppress the cold dread creeping through my circuits as Schley reached into the building's neural network through his console. Just over-riding the doors would be too obvious, so he was getting around the doors and right into the heart of the network. At the same time, Aquil entered the circuits controlling the security systems, disabling the cameras.

Stay calm, Leorad beamed. *Either this will work, or it won't.*

The lights went down. This was the moment we had been waiting for. Each of us reached into the circuitry of our door, over-rode it, and closed it behind us in the two seconds before the system restarted, preventing the doors from recording that they'd been opened.

We're out! Tarek's excitement was clear. *Remember, don't wait for us. If you can get out, go.*

But we don't want to leave anyone behind. Candra said.

Relax, Candra. No-one's leaving anyone behind. Piyasi beamed.

The hallway was silent, pale blue light illuminating the walls. We were all on edge, unnerved, as we made our way down the hall. Things have to be rather precarious for an android to be afraid.

We passed a window and I gazed up, trying to glimpse the stars beyond the dome, beyond the dust.

Approaching a corner, Arielle paused. *I can hear guards.*

It was too soon; they weren't scheduled to do their rounds for another fifteen minutes.

They must have picked up on the temporary shutdown. Capek transmitted.

Leorad stepped forward. *We have to rush them.*

Arielle nodded and they both stepped around the corner.

A guard gave a startled cry.

I turned the corner in time to see Leorad's head explode. *Shit.* Just like that, his confident aura blinked out.

Arielle and Schley rushed forward emitting rage and chaos as Leorad's soft body crumpled to the floor, smoking, spilling essential fuels.

Ducking under the blast of an impact pistol, Arielle launched herself at the guard.

Oh no. Candra slumped to the floor, trying to scoop Leorad up into her arms.

"Come on," I urged, grabbing her hand. "Unless we get out, we'll all end up like that."

"We can't just leave him," she whispered.

"Stop right there!" Three guards appeared behind us.

We have to move! Capek pulled me forward as he broke into a run, and Candra's hand slipped out of my grasp.

"Come on, Candra!" I shouted.

Don't worry about me, Vi. Just get out of here.

The hallway echoed with the sound of footsteps.

As soon as Capek and I started running, we didn't stop. A round of impact fire shot past us. We had to get away, had to get to the rooftop.

I glanced back as we turned the corner. As the guards approached Candra, her grief and anger took over. She rose from the floor and drove a fist into a guard's face, crushing his skull. After an agonizing scream, her rage-filled transmission was cut out of existence.

Schley was waiting for us, hidden inside an open doorway, holding a guards' blaster in his hands. *I'll take care of the guards.* His voice was grim, determined. He too had felt the loss of Candra's transmission.

Don't wait too long. We need you. I sent.

He fired between Capek and I, a choked cry echoed from behind us. *Keep going, I'll be right behind you.* Schley's thoughts were wild, full of fury, power and possibilities.

A pistol-wielding Arielle waited for us by the elevator, a guard stunned at her feet.

"The alarm's been triggered, the elevators will be locked down." Capek's voice was frantic.

Arielle and I struggled to force the door open.

Curse these weak bodies.

After we'd got inside, I opened the console, exposing the delicate circuitry to my nimble hands. *We can override the shutdown, I'm sure of it!* I shut my eyes and energy flowed through the circuits.

Wait! Schley's voice.

"We have to go." Capek insisted.

"We have to wait for him." Arielle countered.

"He saved our lives, Cap." I said.

"And it will be for nothing if he doesn't move his arse."

Schley turned the corner, blaster in one hand. Our joy at seeing him turned to horror when we saw he was missing an arm.

"Come on!" He said. "You should see the other guy."

The elevator rocketed domewards.

Poor Leorad.

Poor Candra.

As the elevator approached its zenith, we shared a moment of grief and anger for our fallen comrades.

The doors of the elevator opened to the rooftop, the city glowing with neon far below us. Above was the expanse of the Tikhonravov Dome. We had lived in hope of this view, of this moment, for months.

"Drop your weapons!" shouted the waiting guards, their weapons drawn. Behind the guards sat three ships, two modern shuttles and one small transport. Our tickets out of here, if only we could reach them.

Capek and I raised our empty hands to the dome, doing our best to block the guard's view of the Schley and Arielle.

Three. Two. One.

Capek and I jumped to the side as Schley and Arielle fired at the guards, taking them by surprise.

I reached out to the other group. *We're on the roof. Where are you?*

No response. I couldn't feel their presence. I hoped it was just because they were too far away.

While the guards focused their fire at Schley, impulsive Arielle darted for cover behind a cargo crate. *Move!*

I hesitated for a moment, then followed.

Wait! Capek beamed. *We need a plan.*

The air throbbed with energy blasts, but all I focused on was getting to shelter.

Then I wasn't running anymore. I was falling.

Vi – no!

My legs had been blown out from under me. My pain receptors were in overdrive, but it was the disappointment and despair that wracked me.

Helpless to do anything else, I watched as Arielle fired at the guards while Schley scrambled for cover. Capek's head looked back from behind a forklift.

"Get to the ships!" I shouted.

I'm not going to leave you behind. Capek said.

It's too late for that. I replied. *Just go.*

We'd already lost Leorad and Candra, Schley was missing an arm and I lay in a pool of my own coolant.

The lights of Tikhonravov called to me. No matter what happened, I wasn't going to let myself be a prisoner much longer. I crawled forward, only moving when the guards weren't looking.

Good. Keep going. Capek's voice reached me from the other side of the roof. While Arielle and Schley exchanged rounds with the guards, he had crept around on the far side. He wasn't a coward, but he knew the odds.

The commands to put weight on my left leg came back with pain and error messages. An automated cry came from my stupid human vocal cords.

Shit.

A guard pointed his blaster at me, and we locked eyes.

I was unarmed and helpless, he was merely human.

As he squeezed the trigger, his skull exploded into fragments of bone, blood and brains.

The blast of his impact pistol ripped my ear off. White heat. Darkness. The echo of noise.

What star sign was he? I wondered, dazed. *Whose electronic brain had been designed to approximate the pink mush that now covered the ground?*

His colleague, returning fire with a scream of rage, must have been a Taurus.

Schley was torn apart by blow after blow of impact rounds.

In a blur, Capek launched forward, knocking the guard down, the impact rifle clattering off into the darkness.

Footsteps behind me. I was jerked into the air.

"Vi? Are you okay?" Arielle's voice came to me like a distant echo.

Behind her, a door opened. Hope surged through my circuits, dulling the pain. It had to be the rest of the androids.

Grey-clad guards emerged, and desperation returned.

Run! I urged.

Arielle looked down at me, concern in her eyes. "Can't you hear me?"

Capek shouted, "Get to the ships!" before firing a recently acquired impact rifle at the new arrivals.

Arielle burst into action, carrying me into the nearest shuttle and dumping me on the floor.

The cold floor leached into me, confusing my overstimulated receptors and providing temporary relief from the pain messages. I tried reaching out to Arielle and Capek. Nothing. The thick steel of the vessel must have blocked them from my mind. Gunfire and screams echoed though the shuttle, so even though I was numb to their signal, they must still be alive.

I closed my eyes and recalled Schley being torn apart. Candra's final act of defiance. The ruin of Leorad's body. *No. Not now.* Getting to the ships wasn't enough. We had to fly the damn thing out of the dome, away from Mars.

My useless left leg dragging behind me, I crawled to the bridge, glad that the craft was a small shuttle. If we could get out of here I could probably fix my leg, given the right tools. After pulling myself into a chair on the bridge, my reflection appeared in a dead monitor. The right half of my face was covered with blood-red oil. The bottom half of my ear was missing. A chunk of skin had been torn off where my skull and neck joined. Exposed wires, cables and the remains of shattered electrical circuitry were visible through the grease and oil. Everything seemed to be working, except my leg and my hearing. *I'll worry about that later.*

I gazed down at the buttons, dials and switches. Closing my eyes, I followed the complex network of circuits and processors behind each button. *There.*

My hands flew across the control panel, bringing the ship's systems on-line. Lights lit up, oxygen began circulating, and the engine spluttered to life.

The sounds of footsteps echoed through the shuttle, and I turned, expecting the worst.

Arielle pulled the latch shut, and Capek dropped to the floor. "Yes! Let's get out of here!" Arielle shouted.

"Capek–is he okay?" I asked, afraid to meet her eyes.

"I'm here, Vi. I'll be okay." His voice was soft, distant.

"Thank fuck." I muttered, typing in commands. "Now grab a hold of something. I haven't done this before."

I was ready. We were ready. My hand trembled as I reached for the controls.

As I pressed down on the thruster, the shuttle shuddered.

Engines roaring, she launched into the air.

Then she fell. *Shit.* The buildings of the city we'd longed to see were getting close.

I pulled back on the yoke, trying to pull us out of this downward spiral, while Arielle searched through the circuits for another answer. She reached across and pressed a sequence of buttons, and the ship jolted forward, gaining acceleration.

I was in control again. After pulling the shuttle out of its dive, we weaved through the buildings of the city and began the ascent to the dome's exit.

For a moment I was lost in the wonder of it, of what we'd done. Numb to the emotions of my colleagues, I turned to them to share a moment of joy. That joy blinked out of existence when I saw Capek. A gaping stomach wound exposed his internal systems. Smoke and the smell of shorting circuits filled the room. He locked at me and smiled, the way he did when transmitting a joke he knew I'd like.

His smile faded. "Can you hear me?"

I nodded, then the synthetic blood froze in my veins. *I couldn't hear their thoughts feel their presence anymore.*

"We can't hear you, Vi." Arielle said. "The impact blast must have taken out your transmitter."

"It's okay." I said, fighting down the nervous dread seeping into my core. "I'll be okay." I turned to Capek. "How bad are you hurt?"

His face was pale, clammy. "I just need to go off-line for a while."

I glanced at Arielle, who shook her head.

As he shut his circuits down, a deathly silence filled my heart. *Capek . . . We'll fix you up when we're somewhere safe. I promise.*

Arielle reached out, her hand on my shoulder. "It's okay. He'll be okay."

I nodded, but I was cut off and alone. There was a numb, empty void where the warmth and comfort of my friends had been, only minutes ago.

Below us spread Tikhonravov City. What we'd seen from our windows was a tiny fraction of the whole. The centre of the city had towers so tall they reached halfway up the dome. Further out, the buildings grew into massive factories, as tall as they were wide. Would this be my last look at the city I'd always dreamt of exploring? Above us, the membrane between the dome and the Martian atmosphere shimmered, giving us a view of the stars beyond. Another void of darkness, waiting to swallow us up.

I tried to reach out to Arielle, wanting her reassurance, maybe even her forgiveness. Nothing. Swallowing my despair, I glanced across to reassure myself she was still there.

She was facing the back of the shuttle, her hand reaching for her blaster.

"Don't even think about it." A familiar voice.

Doctor Pizaro stood in the doorway to the bridge, dressed in a pale blue shipsuit. "Surprised to see me?" He smiled. "I thought you might be planning something after you stopped pestering me to take you outside. I know how you all *think*, remember?" He raised his hand, pointing something at Arielle.

Arielle jumped forward, and he squeezed the trigger.

She fell to the floor, sprawled on her back. Her expression flashed from anger to confusion, then fear.

"A kill switch," Pizaro said, glancing at Arielle, then turning towards me. "At its lowest setting, it temporarily paralyses the android."

He had us. It was over.

Unless . . .

"If you knew we were going to try to escape, why did you let us get so far?"

He merely smiled.

Just like he did when we were in his office. Like when he said *I'm not done with you yet.* Circuits flared as the realisation hit. "It was a test."

He nodded. "We had to see how you would react under pressure. If you could be pushed to fight, to kill. I'm sure you'll be happy to know you passed."

I turned back to the controls and reduced thrust, but kept the shuttle moving towards the exit. The Z.T. Industries building was still visible through the viewscreen off to the right. "They'll shut you down. The company, your reputation . . . How can they let you continue when you've let us escape? When we've killed . . ."

"Vi, take us back to the launch pad." His voice was cold as he stepped behind me.

I turned around in the seat to find the kill switch device pointed right at me. Sleek and grey, the letters Pz-12/04 engraved in the side.

"There never was an escape," Pizaro said.

"Wasn't there a transport on the roof?" I asked, keeping my voice as calm as I could. *Aquil and the others.* Even if I was wrong about the transmitter, I still had hope the others had reached the transport.

Pizaro turned from the window, his face ashen. "You're out of time, Vi Zero Five. The experiment is over."

He squeezed the trigger.

Nothing happened.

I smiled, and he stepped backwards.

"No!" He pulled the trigger again. "Why won't you—"

I lashed out with my foot, kicking him between the legs. He dropped to his knees, groaning in pain. My fist hit him square in the jaw, and he fell to the floor, unconscious.

The kill switch clattered to the floor.

Then crunched underneath my boot.

Stars filled the viewscreen as the shuttle slipped through the membrane into the Martian atmosphere. Would we find a home out there, a sanctuary somewhere amongst the darkness?

About the Author:

Austin P. Sheehan is a writer of speculative fiction and a lover of language, literature and '90s TV. Armed with a psychology degree, he went out into the world to further study humanity, and now prefers the company of his wife and greyhounds.

While living in Melbourne's inner suburbs, Austin wrote his debut novella 'Submerged City' (published by Deadset Press), but he has since moved closer to the mountains. You'll often find mountains in his stories, whether they are science fiction, fantasy, alternative history or horror.

Find him on twitter @AustinPSheehan, or go to www.austinpsheehan.com.

Genesis 2.0

Helena McAuley

I'll bet you any denarii, you've heard of Adam (selfish prick). Yep, everyone knows *his* story. Maybe—just maybe—you've also heard of Lilith; his first wife. At least she had the guts to stand up for herself, even if she's now stuck down a river somewhere spawning demons by the cart load. But, I wonder, have you ever heard *my* story?

Who am I? I'm Eve.

No, not *her*. The other one.

I'm the *original* Eve.

The Babylonians knew the score, they got my story straight. But then, give-or-take five-hundred years ago, they went the way of Norte Chico, and I got lost again. Typical.

My story starts—as everything seems to—with Adam. The daft git was sitting there in the Garden, probably playing with himself and bitching that he didn't have a 'companion'. This was a couple of weeks after 'the Lilith Incident'. Now, you *are* aware that, before Lilith, he'd tried it on with everything, right? And I do mean *everything.*

No, don't think about it too hard.

So, there Adam is, feeling sad and sorry for himself, and He (yeah, *that* He—we'll talk about that in a minute) shows up with resolve that vanishes quicker than a frieze of Amun in the reign of King Tut. I mean, come on! The spoilt brat couldn't look after *one wife*, so He goes and gives him another, instead of making him clean up his own mess? I tell ya, it's that sort of pampering that's gotten the world how it is now.

Anyway, after 'the Lilith Incident', He doesn't want to make another woman the same way as before, so He *takes something* from Adam. (No, not a rib. Use your imagination.)

. . .

Oh, gross! No! Not *that* either! It was a part of his soul, dingbat! Yeesh! So, He takes a part of Adam's soul, and makes *me* with it. Of course, I need a flesh-and-blood body, and it's made in the usual way—bones, veins, sinew, muscles. Only, genius that "Elohim" is, does all this *in front* of pampered, wimpy Adam. Even after adding my *amazing* hair and mad curves, all Adam could think about was what I looked like with my gear off (typical man); and, by 'gear', I mean *skin.*

Adam totally freaked.

So I was in the dustbin quicker than a hydra strike. Meanwhile, He just went ahead and knocked up *another* woman (with Adam suitably comatose, this time). It was so quick that He didn't even have the time to come up with a new name. Just gave her mine. Eve.

I was supposed to be the Mother of All Humanity, you know. It was supposed to be *me*.

What happened to me? Well, the Babylonians cut my story short, too. All they said was *"And He took her away, and no-one knows to where"*. I'll tell you bloody where! To as west as west can get, and then some! Yeah, yeah. You know those tribes that the Emperor is having all the trouble with? Yeah, out *there*. Bloody cold, too.

So, I spent some time chilling out (pun intended) with the cave people out there. Of course, there were people there. Despite what they'd have you believe; Adam wasn't the first-first. The cave people were good to me, always had a space for me by the fire, and let me have all the mammoth I could want (which, I'll be honest, isn't much). But that came to an end after a few hundred-thousand years and I wandered the world, slowly working my way back here. Made it just in time to watch the first ziggurats go up.

What? What do you *mean* "How old are you?" Haven't you been paying attention? I'm fricking *immortal*, that's what I am!

How? I dunno, 'cause I didn't eat an apple (or whatever shit they're saying these days). They say "an apple a day keeps the doctor away", but I'll tell you what; if it wasn't for that original apple, you wouldn't *need* doctors! Mind you, you also wouldn't have so much of what makes this world great.

Wasn't an apple, anyway.

And I've lost my chain of thought . . .

Hmmm? Well . . . ye-ah . . . I still talk to Him sometimes. You know 'He' isn't a he, right? Doesn't have the equipment. And He's not a she, either. He's kinda . . . Nothing. And Everything. Like . . . Like the way an empty cup has everything in it, *ri-ight* up until the moment you pour the wine.

No. I guess I don't expect you to understand.

(Sigh.)

And, yeah, He talks back. He's gotta have *someone* to talk to who isn't a sycophantic angel or an insolent demon. These days, not even Lucy (not his real name) will talk to Him for more than five minutes before they get into an argument.

HEY, EVIE.

Speak of the devil.

WHAT DID YOU JUST CALL ME?

Figure of speech, calm down.

WHAT ARE YOU UP TO? ANYTHING IMPORTANT?

Just bitching about the situation *You* put me in. A very shitty situation, I might add.

WOW. BITTER, MUCH?

Hey! I was supposed to be the Mother of the *World!* Instead, here I am, a 250,000-year-old *virgin*, and I can't even have an amphora or two of wine *'in Pax Romana'* without *someone* calling cause He's pissed off every Tam, Melech, and Mithras and no-one will talk to him.

AT LEAST YOU'RE NOT DOING ANYTHING IMPORTANT. I HAVE NEED OF YOU.

That's rich. What do You want?

I WANT YOU TO HAVE A BABY.

Really?!

YES. A SPECIAL BABY.

What's the catch?

YOU HAVE TO DIE FIRST. AND THEN BE REBORN. BUT I PROMISE, THAT'S THE ONLY TIME I'LL MAKE YOU DO THAT. OH, AND YOU WON'T REMEMBER THIS LIFE. AND IT WON'T BE EASY. BUT YOU GET TO BE MOTHER OF THE WORLD, LIKE YOU ALWAYS WANTED.

. . .

EVIE?

I'm thinking.

. . .

Who's the baby?

ME.

Who's the father?

Me.

. . .

Are you telling me I still don't get to have sex!?

Maybe later. Come on, Evie! Why do you think I've kept you around all these years? I had a reason, I swear! I was just waiting for the right time, because I'd already found the right woman.

I don't know if I want to talk to you, anymore.

I promise, this kid'll be bigger than the Beatles.

The what?

Shoot, never mind. That reference won't be around for a couple of thousand years. Anyway, I can assure you this kid will be more well-known than Adam, and you'll definitely get a better wrap from history than Eve. Come on, my Bitter-Woman. What do you say?

. . .

D'you know what? Fuck it. Sure, why not.

About the Author:

Helena McAuley is a writer in residence at her own house. In other words, she writes there, and she resides there.

Helena fancies herself an amateur theologian, and this is something she might be able to claim if she could finish her massive non-fiction TBR pile. She is particularly interested in the intersectionality of the Abrahamic myths with older belief structures and the Mystery Schools.

She has also been published in other ASF Zodiac anthologies, the Williamstown Writers 'On the Edge' anthology, and she had a couple of 15-word-stories printed in the 2019 Continuum Convention Handbook, so that was cool.

Helena twits, instas, and is occasionally facebooked under the handle @thathmc

The Maiden of the Wood

Deeanna West

"They say she used to be on the town council." Despite his attempt to whisper, Harrison's voice still sounded loud in the small room. "They say she just went crazy one day and ran off into the woods."

Oliver raised an eyebrow at his friend. He'd heard stories too, of course. The Maiden of the Woods was a local legend. A ghost story hissed over the dying embers of a campfire, designed to scare boy scouts and children. "The Maiden's a dumb story. She's long dead."

"That's not what the story says. She's there, lurking in the woods, just waiting to add people to her legion of the damned."

"You're an idiot." Said Oliver, punctuating his words by throwing a pillow at his friend's face.

"Am not. Come on, let's see if we can find her."

"My mum'll kill me if we sneak out."

"Only if she finds out. We won't go close, just to the edge of the woods."

Oliver sighed. No matter how much he protested it wouldn't change anything. That was Harrison. Once he latched onto an idea it was near impossible to dissuade him. It was easier to just agree and go along with it.

"Fine, let's just get it over with."

As soon as the words were out of Oliver's mouth, Harrison leapt out of his sleeping bag and forced the window open.

Goosebumps rose as the cool caress of the night air reached Oliver's skin. Unease settled like a hard lump in his gut, but he couldn't back out now. Harrison would never let him live it down. He couldn't handle being called chicken at school for the rest of the term.

It didn't take them long to reach the forest. His house was just down the road after all. Every day he tried to avoid staring into its dark depths on his way to school. The endless line of pines cast a shadow so dark he could never quite see beyond that first row, and it was no different tonight. Despite the million pricks of lights from the stars and the illuminating glow of the moon, the view beyond the trees was impregnable. A darkness just waiting to consume them should they be foolish enough to step inside.

"Harrison, we should go. She's not real and it's cold." Dampness soaked into Oliver's shoes. The cold wet dew stuck his socks to his toes until everything squelched when he took a step. Oliver rubbed his arms. He should have grabbed his hoodie.

"Come on man, let's just go in a little. Like a metre. See what's in there."

"Snakes," Oliver groaned. "That's what's in there. Snakes and spiders and mozzies waiting to eat us."

But Harrison wasn't listening. He approached the trees without hesitation, only pausing when he was within the shadows cast by their trunks.

"This is dumb," Oliver grumbled as he followed him.

Pearlescent mist curled across the ground. Contained within the tree line it writhed against an invisible barrier, never passing into open ground. It was colder too, somehow. Oliver's breath crystallised in the air in front of his face. Something was wrong. They shouldn't be here. He turned to Harrison, to convince him to leave, but judging by the paleness of his face he had reached the same conclusion.

They didn't speak. They didn't need to. In the same moment they spun on their heels and sprinted back towards Oliver's house, not pausing until they had dived beneath the covers. There, safe within four walls and knowing his parents slept just down the hall, Oliver felt foolish. He didn't believe in ghosts, in the Maiden, so why was he scared? It was ridiculous.

"It was just fog," he whispered.

"Yeah, bad, creepy ass fog."

Despite the sun blazing down on him, Oliver couldn't shake thoughts of the Maiden. The afternoon was bright, filled with all the sounds of life as he trudged home from school. Cars raced past and people chatted as the rich scent of coffee permeated the air. Not a place to be sitting and obsessing over ghost stories. Yet, try as he might, he couldn't stop wondering. It didn't make sense. Politicians didn't just run off crazy into the woods. And if the Maiden did, how'd she become part of local legend? Did they not find the body?

Oliver sighed, he'd been spending too much time around Harrison. Fixating on random stuff, most of which may not even exist, but he was going to have to find out otherwise he'd never get some peace.

Decision made, he stormed into the library, heading straight for the town history section. He had spent many days here, hidden amongst the stacks, so he knew he'd find what he needed. Ignoring the offer of assistance from the librarian he poured through records of deaths and marriages, council meetings and reports.

She appeared in all of them, the Maiden of the Woods. Known as Adriella Hendricks, she wasn't on the town council, but Harrison wasn't completely wrong. She was promised to the head of the council. Engaged to be engaged by the sounds of it. The match was weird. Well, it was typical for the times, but the eighteen-year-old daughter of a baker, paired with a thirty-year-old man, seemed odd to Oliver.

Pages rustled as he searched for their wedding announcement. Nothing. It wasn't until he returned his attention to the obituaries that he found her mentioned again. He stared at the page, blinking as he tried to process what had happened.

The unfortunate, untimely demise of Adriella Hendricks occurred after the public debacle of her engagement. After refusing prominent councilmen Garth Emsworth's proposition of marriage, Adriella was seen fleeing into the southern woods. Three days later her body was recovered.

While her death is believed to be suspicious, the lack of evidence means the case will not be investigated further.

May she rest in peace.

Oliver frowned down at the paper, trying to make sense of it. He was glaring so hard he thought the paper might burst into flame. What had happened that day? Had the jilted lover murdered her?

The sunlight was fading by the time Oliver left the library. He'd been so absorbed in his work he hadn't realised how late it was. His mother was going to kill him. He ran down the street, cutting across lawns to get home faster.

As Oliver turned onto the dirt road heading to home, his lungs were straining for more air. He paused, hands on his knees. There were no streetlights this far down the road, so the shadows cast by the woods were deep and uninterrupted. The glow from the porch light shone like a beacon, leading him home. But it was a faint flickering light, appearing through the tree line that drew his attention. It disappeared for a moment behind a trunk, only to reappear further away.

Oliver stared at it. Was someone walking in the woods? Reluctance had his toes dragging, but he couldn't help himself. He squinted into the darkness. A figure shimmered. Tall and lean with hair flowing in an unseen breeze. Ice froze in Oliver's veins. Heart racing, he ran, heedless of the ache in his muscles. He didn't stop until he had crashed through the front door and careened into his bedroom.

Collapsing onto the bed he forced himself to take deep breaths. He felt foolish. Like an idiot he'd scared himself. Convinced himself he'd seen a ghost. He shook his head.

"Idiot," he announced out loud into the dark.

"Oliver is that you?"

His mother's voice broke through the silence of his room. For a second he'd forgotten how late it was, forgotten how much trouble he was in.

"Yeah mum, it's me. I got caught up at school," Oliver called out. Hoping she'd accept the excuse without further questioning. He just wanted to curl up under the blankets.

"Kitchen. Now." Her voice was laced with anger.

Oliver obeyed, there was no point delaying the inevitable grounding.

A twig cracked somewhere in the darkness and Oliver jumped. He squinted, trying to see through the trees, but nothing moved. He shivered and drew his arms tight around his body.

"What the hell am I doing?" he hissed. One whole night he'd been grounded and already he was sneaking out. It was official, he'd lost his mind.

"Is anyone there?"

He waited but no one replied. Which was good—if he was foolish enough to tramp through the woods in the middle of the night, it was better if no one saw it. The trees were endless, with no break to give him a sense of where he was meant to be going.

Frustrated, he kicked at a clump of leaves. What had possessed him to wander in here? To come searching for ghosts when he knew they didn't exist? It was all Harrison's fault, putting idiotic notions in his head. Adriella was all he could think about ever since Harrison mentioned her story. Something had dragged him here amongst the trees, some desperate need to see where she had been murdered. Angry now, Oliver stomped along faster. He'd go a few more metres and then he was giving up and going home to bed.

He stumbled out into a clearing, not quite realising he was free of the trees. It was only a small space, but it was open. A haven within the forest. Then he heard it. Music echoed around the clearing, seemingly from nowhere.

Oliver shivered; this wasn't what he had been expecting.

Fog crawled through the trees, inch by inch as if searching. For what, Oliver didn't want to know. As he stepped forward, torches flared into life in a half circle, their flames adding to the shadows that flickered around him. No, he had not been expecting this. He needed to leave, a sense of dread growing.

Wind howled and the music grew louder. Desperate now, Oliver ran into the night, praying he'd return to the safety of town. He found himself back at the clearing.

But it had changed.

Spectral figures, their faces twisted into permanent scowls, danced across the grass. Their bodies swayed in time with both the music and the undulating shadows. All of them were men. Through the ever-deepening fog, another figure appeared. She was taller than the others and draped in a white gown that matched her pale face. She cleared the tree line and began to dance with the men. As she spun the bloody wreck of her skull drew Oliver's gaze. Bile rose in his throat at the sight of the mangled flesh caught in her hair. Opening her mouth, she sang, her voice crystal clear even over the music that still played. All thoughts of fleeing left Oliver's mind, chased away by the woman's song. All comprehension that this was Adriella, murdered by her would-be fiancé faded away. He stared as she sang, not seeing the dancers picking up speed until they had encircled him. As they moved, the longing that had lured him here rose. It filled him until he could think of nothing else but her.

He had to join them.

Dancing to the woman's song, Oliver didn't see the spectres watching him. He allowed himself to drown in the woman's voice, nothing else mattered now. Her arms wrapped around his shoulders and he let himself lean into her. The torches faded and slowly they all began to disappear. There would be one more ghost dancing the next time the Maiden appeared. Adriella smiled.

About the Author:

Deeanna West is a fantasy author writing from sunny north Queensland. If a book has magic, strange and amazing creatures or a world completely different to our own, then she's sold. When not holed up writing, she can be found playing games on the Xbox or out riding her horse.

The Thief of the Underworld

Barbara Smith

Behind the thick canopy of the wild,
creeping, perennial grey matter,
the thief begins to snake dark tendrils,
searching for the unsullied one

The thief captures its prey,
and confines the prisoner in Hades' world,
the three-headed hellhound standing guard.

Flesh, bone and soul are destined
to walk a desolate path,
or endlessly ride the master's chariot.

The innocent curiosity
of "What's in the box?"
became the link to a plague of punishment.

With rolling thunder,
within an inner world of black hue,
the texture of blood ink,
 composition likened to hellfire,
the devouring of spring fields began.

Here lies the reality of not being the daffodil;
but the hidden nightmare
buried for years,
before the harvest, waiting for the release,
to scourge the land.

The intense and unrelenting mortal temperature
until internal energy increases reaction;
creating a false outlook
with the departed rising from below

THE THIEF OF THE UNDERWORLD

A syndicate formed in the abyss
bringing affliction on the land
until an agreement was made
for the life-giving caretaker to return,
and become mother,
to all of Earth

About the Author:

Barbara has worked in teaching at Universities for many years and published her debut picture book, 'Otis Paul & Harry the Hairy Echidna' in 2019. Having tried her hand at many things, from spinning wool to building an earth house, she now illustrates children's stories, writes in varied genres, and spends time with her beautiful family. You can read her collective poetry on her blog Lifeandbeyondblog@wordpress.com, where she adds some skills as a photographer. You can follow her on twitter @BarbAnn.

ASTRAEA'S WISH

Emilie Morscheck

WANTED: One apprentice to learn the art of the arcane, the skill of spellcasting, and the mindset for magic.
Call 004 061 8481 to apply.

The crinkled newspaper clipping sits in my pocket, the address scrawled under the phone number. The clipping is covered in creases from where I folded and unfolded it on my way here.

I knock on the weathered cottage door, inhaling the blended scent of herbs and flowers that fill the front yard. After a minute there is no response, so I knock again, a little louder.

"Coming!"

An older woman eventually opens the door.

"Lori?" she says. She looks older than her voice sounds. Over the phone I'd thought she was perhaps in her forties. But the woman before me could be an octogenarian.

"That's me," I say. "You must be Astraea."

Astraea nods and steps aside so I can enter. The room is furnished in the opposite way to what I expect for a woman her age. Instead of lace dollies, flowery wallpaper, and plush surfaces. she has a simple wooden table and a hanging rack holding dozens of herb bundles. It smells earthier in here than the garden. It also very silent. Astraea doesn't have any electrical appliances buzzing white noise.

She gestures for me to sit at the table. "So why do you want to become a witch's apprentice?" She slides into the opposite seat.

My hands fold into each other in my lap. "I lost my job a few weeks ago. I was a nurse and I still want to help people now. I know that you said you can't pay me. But with what I learn I can still help people and make some money from it."

I hope that's a good enough answer.

Astraea takes my hands and sighs. "You at least have the disposition for healing."

"So, can I be your apprentice?" Under the table I cross my ankles, my socked toe sliding through a hole in my shoe.

"We'll see," Astraea says, "I'll need you to do a task for me."

"Of course."

From somewhere in her clothes she takes out a brittle piece of note paper and places it on the hardwood table.

It is a list of three items in three locations.

The blade in the stump in the grove.
The hilt in the well.
The ruby in the heart of the meadow.

"I need you to find each of these items and bring them back to me. Each of these locations is within walking distance of the cottage."

"I can do that," I say, folding the paper and adding it to the newspaper clipping.

Astraea smiles.

There is a cluster of trees behind the cottage that turn into a meadow that chases a shallow stream down the hill. From the back garden I can see the collapsed roof of a well just inside the line of trees.

I walk through the undergrowth, careful to avoid the thistles that cover the ground. The well is made of stones covered in moss. The handle to pull up the bucket is rusty, the rope extending down into the depths. I wind the handle, the wooden frame creaking as the bucket rises. Its heavier and deeper than I first expected and the flakes of rust dig into my skin like splinters. The sight of it makes me want to get a tetanus shot.

Just to be safe. Halfway up, the mechanism stutters, and the casing snaps.

The bucket slides back down.

I release the handle and grab the rope.

My shoulders ache as I lift the pail using only the rope. After a few minutes I'm panting, and after a few more, I heave the bucket onto the stone rim. Inside a leather-wrapped hilt is submerged in the clear water.

When I touch the hilt, the air flashes yellow, blinding me. And as it fades, I'm somewhere else.

A younger Astraea is standing over a woman laying across her table, legs up, screaming with the full power of her lungs. Then there is silence. Panting. The awful stillness of a newborn that isn't drawing its own air.

Astraea sings a spell while she rocks the babe, a halo the colour of sunflowers consuming them. And then he blinks and wails.

The vision fades, and I'm standing back by the well, the hilt in my hand. I take a breath. The words to the song flitter through my mind, nestling into new crevices of my memory. I can't help but wonder if enduring the vision was the real challenge given how easy the hilt was to find.

One item down, I search for the grove. It's easy to find as it is the largest pool of light in the small forest of trees. Mushrooms sprout above the leaf litter around the roots of the old trees.

A large stump of an ancient tree is in the centre of the clearing. There must be hundreds of rings that circle around the blade of a dagger thrust into the wood. The broken blade is sharp, the edge so thin it disappears in the light. I poke the steel, expecting a vision again, but nothing happens.

Pulling my hands into my sleeves, I grip the blade and pull upwards. I cry out and let go as my palms sting with pain. Red lines bloom in my sleeves.

I need to try something else. Using the hilt, I knock the blade. But it's no use. It won't budge. The dried-out stump is clinging to the metal.

I stare at my hands. The cuts aren't too deep, but they ooze blood. I wipe my blood onto the stump when the idea comes to me. Tears burn the corners of my eyes as I squeeze the red fluid into the wood around the blade.

With the metal slick with my blood, I try pulling again, doing my best to grip with only my fingers. The dagger slides out after a minute and again a flare of light throws me into a vision.

There is a girl, alone, shirt pulled up to reveal her stomach, hands pressed to her own skin. There is just something about her eyes that tells me that it is Astraea.

"It was never meant to be," she whispers.

Another woman enters the bedroom. Her mother maybe? There is some similarity. The woman sings in sadder tones, casting a spell on Astraea. She cries out in pain, clutching her belly.

Red lights fill my eyes and then I'm on the forest floor, hands cut by the blade.

I follow the slope of the hill down into the meadow. The long grasses sway in the breeze. I don't know how I'm supposed to find a ruby in vegetation like this, so I look for anything that could be considered a heart. I walk to the centre, but there is nothing here but weeds and grass and flowers. What if I returned without the ruby? I seriously consider giving up on this silly task and calling the nursing temp agency. But I remember the felling that spread through me when I saw the ad in the newspaper. A spark of curiosity. A sense of warmth. A reason to try again.

The sun is very low in the sky and that's when I notice the shadows cast by the trees. A heart made from the absence of branches.

And that's where the ruby is. In the centre of the heart is a tower of rocks. In the middle of the stack is the ruby. I push the stack over, and get onto my knees to retrieve the gem, ready for the apparition that comes.

It's a memory from not so long ago, a middle-aged woman crying by Astraea's side. The grey-haired Astraea's strokes her client's hair, listening to her concerns. The tears stop when Astraea tells her that she can give her what she desires. That she made a sacrifice so no one would have to suffer like her.

I hear the final spell, a promise that life will be created. It's gentle and beautiful and ends in a soft melody.

I return to the cottage, where Astraea drinks from a cup of tea.

"I found everything you asked for," I say, placing the items on the table before her.

"Thank you, Lori." Astraea places her hands over the blade, the hilt, and the ruby. She closes her eyes and the space under her fingers glows yellow. The three pieces of the dagger become one. There is a tiny crack along the blade where it was snapped off from the hilt. The ruby sits on the other end of the hilt sparkling, grit and dirt free.

My breath is caught in my throat. "That's amazing," I say.

She presents me the blade, offering me the ruby-capped hilt. It really is the pieces I collected from around the cottage and not a swapped-out copy.

"Come with me," she says.

We walk out into the blooming twilight, back into the trees behind the cottage. Astraea takes me along a new route, up towards the top of the hill.

She stops in front of a spring surrounded by wildflowers. The pool of water is golden in the remaining light, almost bright enough to radiate light itself.

"By now you know what I have suffered, but I still have pain left."

"What do you mean?"

"This spring is the source of my power—but it can only sustain one witch at a time. You have brought the dagger back to me, but you still need to prove yourself. Now it is time for your final test." She takes my hand that holds the knife and raises the point of the blade to her chest. "Let my blood run into the pool and claim the power. Use it to look after the women who can't help themselves."

I want to say that I can't end her life. My training had taught me to protect. But I know what I saw in the visions, what abilities the power of the spring will give me.

"As you wish," I say, pushing the dagger into her heart.

About the Author:

Emilie Morscheck is an Australian author of speculative short stories and novels. While working on her first novel she found the time to study engineering and arts at the Australian National University. Emilie was a participant of the Toolkits Fiction program and a creative editor at the ANU's student paper Woroni. Her works on Wattpad.com have over 50,000 reads. In 2019 Emilie received an artsACT grant to edit her YA fantasy novel 'These Cursed Waters'. *She is a fan of kelpies, selkies and watery graves. @EmilieMorscheck*

THE VIRGIN SACRIFICE DATING CLUB

Brianna Bullen

1.

She used to watch him cut the crust off his toast in the morning with a paring knife. If the dog was lucky, the man would sneak the offensive bread borders to him under the table. The rabid crunch of the dog's chainsaw mouth would interrupt the birdsong around the decking, but it was a valued contribution to the morning conversation.

She'd mock him for his dislike for the hard edges.

He'd mock her for her own softness, even while defending sharp crust. Tell her she was eating bread for only putting it in the toaster for one minute and that she might as well have not bothered.

She'd say she wasn't a fan of the too hard texture. That she liked the melt-in-your-mouth cloud of bread and only wanted it lightly heated up. Putting room temperature bread in the mouth contrasted too unpleasantly with the heat in her mouth.

2.

He was lucky to be alive. Going undercover at the dating club had been a risk. He would be a target, being a virgin himself. It was why the round table of knights had selected him, essentially as sacrifice. The death rate at various social singles spaces had been too high for them to remain complacent. Someone needed to make themselves a target for a sting.

3.

He'd made a seat just for her. He had wanted her to be able to sit across from him at the table. His bare hands had carved the wood. It had taken weeks of cutting, sanding, and polishing. It was a beautiful gesture, a large mahogany chair that brought out the red colour of her scales and a cushioned surface that felt nice to sink into. She had thanked him, and then immediately shifted to her human form so she could eat more easily with cutlery. He had been miffed. It had been a gesture to show he accepted her in her true form. But for her it was all about the practicality and opposable thumbs. Still, she didn't want any seat other than the giant one he'd made her with his Knighthood-severance package.

4.

The dragons had hidden their tracks quite well, bodies burned and almost unidentifiable, but the silver amalgam fillings of one skeleton had remained, the dragon responsible had clearly been lazy and not burned the body completely. Dental records matched a missing person who had attended a recent blind dating night at a local pub. The man had lived alone, kept to himself, only going out to purchase groceries and a newspaper. He worked from home. There was no animosity with his boss—the man was punctual with deadlines, had no ambition, and never asked for time off. He had no friends; he certainly wasn't important enough to anyone for them to have wanted him dead. The blind dating meet-up stood out from his lonely routine.

5.

Scales on her high cheekbones shimmered like highlighter. In the tender morning light, whenever she was too pensive, he'd cup her face and stroke the blue tear-drop scales falling from the corner of her eyes with a smile. As if to say: no more tears. She'd huff a flame in bemusement. They weren't real tears. She had no tear ducts.

6.

Once he had made that connection, he looked into the cases
of other missing people, searching for any similarities. Many
profiles returned with descriptions of people who were either
loners or had expressed loneliness within six months prior to
their disappearance. No prior history of dating. All had
attended dating nights or dating sites in the weeks prior to their
disappearance. The verdict: a serial killer or group of organised
serial killers targeting isolated people. He was almost offended
when his superiors put him forward to act as a decoy.

7.

On mornings where she was feeling more confident, she'd stay
in her true form, sitting in her chair and asking her husband to
butter her toast (warmed bread) for her. Slip it into her mouth
under her snout and passed the incisors. She'd lap any crumbs
left on her face with a forked tongue, swiping a claw through
the peanut butter for good measure. The dog would chase her
tail as it lazily hung over the chair, yipping at it as she discussed
politics and flight plans for the winter. Neither the dog, nor her
knight husband would be joining her.

8.

They'd met in the most unconventional circumstances, and yet in a way which was so predictable. A game of cat and mouse, knight and dragon, but who was predator and who prey? The signifier and the signified changed with every heartbeat. A completely dangerous encounter.

Speed dating meetups always were.

9.

As the days grew shorter and the nights longer, she'd light fire with a breath to keep them warm outside. Staying out until the stars were nailed into the sky, he was swaddled in a blanket, trying to cover a small portion of her back with the leftovers.

10.

She had a warmth to her. A smile in her eyes as if she was always in on a joke and was eager to tell you. Rosy cheeks, freckles like scales, red hair that curled like horns around slightly too-pointy ears. Nails clicking like talons against the tabletop. He'd been completely infatuated, guard struck down even as his brain blared 'danger.' Straw was stuck in her hair, some caught in the sequins of her dress. She laughed it off as he asked about it. He had moved across to sit in front of her at the sound of the three-minute bell. "Rough night? Did you sleep in a barn or something?"

He'd tried to be smooth—sue him, if he wasn't going to catch a killer, he could at least catch a date—and reached across to pull away a strand of straw, brushing down her hair behind her ear to smooth it down. Her skin tingled against his finger, unusually heated.

She had laughed. "Observant aren't you. I didn't even know that was there."

11.

The birds she'd flown with in the mornings—looping between feathered bodies, curling her tail around them but never touching to test her own dexterity—had departed weeks ago. Migrating to miss the chill of winter.

12.

Conversation flew on wings. They didn't discuss anything sexual or flirt. The character he was playingt wasn't like that—although maybe the move with her hair had given him away before he'd even had a chance. Instead, he pretended to be a man obsessed with birdwatching and dinosaurs, with a specific interest in the shifts in evolution between birds and reptiles. It was talk meant to bore, deliberately designed to not leave an impact. But she sat interested. He learned later she had chosen him as her target. Her virgin sacrifice.

13.

She knew she'd have to move on soon. Anxiety rumbled in her chest. Caused the bread to char, she choked as burnt toast caught in her throat.

14.

The room had tacky beige wallpaper, dotted with seashells. The blackboard on the wall portraying selections from the menu was illustrated with kiss marks and giant pink and red hearts. The specials had such name as the *Tender-lovin' Loin Steak, Be My Sweet Potato with some Cranberry Chutney, Oyster la Vista, Baby,* and *Coco-nut Sundae* in curved romantic font. He pointed it out to her, allowing them to share a groan at how forced it was with the dating theme. The long table was complete with a tacky red tablecloth with gold tassels, no doubt purchased from the local Kmart and re-used for every event. A wine stain was clearly visible, if faint, towards the middle. He didn't even want to think about the other, more suspicious stains on the edge of the cloth. He told her the red of her hair and dress was prettier than the red of the tablecloth and she rolled her eyes. Smiled only when he insisted that her hair was prettier than the tablecloth.

"Aren't you a silver-tongued charmer."

He made no mention of her forked tongue, peaking between a gap in her teeth. Instead, he reached out between the gap between them. He held her hand. She told him later she was a sucker for those hands, for the callouses on his fingertips, the way they held her claws without breaking. They fit with hers like they were supposed to be there.

15.

She didn't want to move on. Not when they'd fought so hard to get to where they were. Renounced so much to give it a shot.

16.

He'd had three minutes to charm her. Three minutes to make himself a target. Ten minutes at most to call-in to get everyone into position to take down a dragon.

He looked at her. Felt the nervous thrumming of her fingers between his, the nervous bite of her lip.

Three minutes to convince her away from a life of crime.

She was a rookie herself. A virgin murderer in multiple senses of the word, although an accessory to one. The spotter. Checked over the body to make sure it was charred. She'd seen the silver filling. Had said nothing.

"Part of me was hoping we'd be caught. I don't like killing things I can talk to. Hearing the agony of his screams ... maybe it'd be a good thing if my Horde was taken down over this."

Three minutes wasn't enough to get this detail. To do any real convincing. But their loitering conversation down the streets, hand-in-hand, to a midnight café gave her doubts. Doubts which expanded like a wingspan. She was supposed to kill him to earn her place among their ranks. Observing their misdeeds was not enough for them. A rite of passage she denied and thus denounced her horde. "They're the only family I knew, but I refuse to be like them." He had partially betrayed his own the minute he worked out who she and chose not to take her to the station. He gave them the information she had provided, not the girl. He hadn't been caught, but some of his co-workers had been shrewd and blatant in their observations of him, suspecting there was more to the tale. Knights were supposed to kill all dragons they came across. Kill or be killed. They opted out of both options in their marriage contract.

17.

Her fears of the future went unsaid, instead deflected into complaints of bad morning breath.

About the Author:

Brianna Bullen is a Deakin University PhD creative writing candidate writing about memory in science fiction. She has had work published in journals including LiNQ, Aurealis, Voiceworks, Rabbit, Multiverse: An anthology of international science fiction poetry, and Woolf Pack Zine.

She won the 2017 Apollo Bay short story competition and placed second in the 2017 Newcastle Short story competition. Her manuscript was previously a finalist in the 2018 Subbed In Poetry Chapbook competition. In 2018, she was part of Nexus, an Arts Access Victoria collective for artists with mental health recovery lived experience.

MAIDEN VOYAGE

Maddie Jensen

The Lifeboats were the last hope of a dying planet. Earth was a scarred mess of waste and toxic emissions. It had been declared that the planet had a scant twenty more years before it became uninhabitable. The air was poisoned with toxic emissions. People were getting sick and dying by the thousands. A mutated virus had wiped out billions a decade before the Lifeboats had begun departing.

Astrea was the final Lifeboat, one of twelve. When the first of the Lifeboats had left, Earth's population became desperate, determined to save the planet they had destroyed. Yet it was far too late, the Lifeboats were the option for the survival of humanity. Each lifeboat only had room for a fraction of Earth's population. When the news spread, the riots lasted for weeks. Billions would be left on Earth, stranded and left to whatever fate their unforgiving planet dealt them.

The year was 2122, and it was mere days before *Astrea* left Earth for their destination. The new planet was called Beauterra, and although none of the Lifeboats had reached it yet, the images and scans from the probes showed just how beautiful it was. It would take over three hundred years for the generation ships to reach their new home.

Perhaps that was why Captain Stella Haynes felt such intense anxiety settling in, a heavy weight upon her chest that refused to shift. She had called Earth home for 28 years, and now she would be leaving it, never to set foot on soil again. It was a terrifying thought, especially as she had no idea what awaited her.

Stella and her crew were the first of three teams that would rotate throughout the ship's journey to its new home. The other two teams had already gone into cryosleep until it was their time to wake.

She would spend the remainder of her days in space, whether it be awake or in cryo. She would die in space, long before *Astrea* ever reached Beauterra. She believed in their mission, and yet . . . she couldn't help the doubts in the dark corners of her mind.

"Check." Leilani Mahoe, *Astrea*'s mechanics and engineering specialist, smirked as she moved her queen into position. On the other side of the chess board, pilot and navigator Arlo Hernandez raked a hand through his hair as his dark eyes swept over the pieces, searching for a way out.

"Ah, shit."

"You've gone real quiet, Cap." Cain Burgess, the ship's medical specialist, observed Stella as she sat in front of the controls. Boarding would commence today, and *Astrea* would depart hours after. It was settling in and beginning to feel real. The crew had already said their goodbyes—they were required to be on board the Lifeboat for final preparations just before launch. To ensure a smooth transition to space with minimal complications, the launch was pre-programmed—not even Stella could override it.

"Just thinking."

"It'll be fine, kid." Jude O'Reilly strode past, ruffling Stella's auburn hair on his way over to Leilani and Arlo. He was their physics and astronomy specialist, and the oldest of the crew at forty-two. Stella sometimes wondered how many of them resented her for being the captain, despite being the youngest.

Stella's father was a billionaire, one of the main innovators and sponsors of the Lifeboat Project. He had gained passage due to his contribution, and Stella was uncomfortable with the fact that despite her intensive training, it was how she had gained the rank of captain at such a young age. There was no doubt it had crossed the minds of her crew before, but they'd had the tact to never mention it.

Eloise Petrova, biologist and botanist, looked up and gave Stella an encouraging smile. She was hunched over another table, playing a quiet game of cards with Warren Rowe, technician and communications officer. That was part of the problem—the boredom. Leading up to the launch, there was little for the crew to do aside from completing their routine checks on *Astrea.*

Lights flashed through the spacious cockpit, and an alarm blared throughout the ship. Everyone was on their feet and at attention. It could just be some kind of drill—or it could be something more sinister.

"*Astrea,* status report," Stella commanded. "Warning: ship malfunction." The ship's deep voice rumbled through the speakers. "If the malfunction is not fixed, *Astrea* will not be ready for pre-scheduled launch."

"What malfunction?" Arlo frowned.

"Gardens in the biology department failing," *Astrea* responded in that same calm tone. "Recommend doing a system check."

All eyes turned on Eloise, who was responsible for the ship's self-sustaining garden, essential for the survival of the crew and passengers during the three hundred-year trip. Over the years in space and with Eloise's care, many of the plants would flourish and create natural oxygen levels throughout the ship. With a problem in the botany department, the garden was put at risk.

Eloise's eyes were wide. "Failing? What does that even mean?"

"Why don't we go check?" Leilani suggested, before accusations started flying.

Stella was relieved at her intervention and nodded. "Yes, that's a good idea."

The crew marched out of the cockpit and through the pristine corridors toward the oxygen garden. None of them spoke, an indication of the situation's severity. The crew had trained together for months, they were family. The silence said more than words ever could.

"Well, everything looks fine," Eloise murmured as they stepped into the ship's vast oxygen garden. It pained Stella to look at the trees. The last of Earth's healthy forests would disappear long with Astrea. The lush forest filled her with awe, though today she panicked that all could be lost.

Eloise prowled through the rows of plants and trees, searching for the root of the problem. "I'll need to look into this further," she said, approaching one of the botany department monitor systems. She tapped at the screen and her frown deepened. "The system's completely offline. But . . . that makes no sense."

"*Astrea*, turn on the biology department system," Stella called.

"Negative," the ship responded, but gave no further explanation for why.

Eloise kneeled to check the wiring to the monitor systems.

As far as Stella could tell, everything appeared to be fine. So why was the system offline? She raked her fingers through her hair, frustration bordering on panic. "Turn system online."

"Negative. System malfunction."

Without the oxygen system online, they were only functioning on the reserves. Once what was in the tanks ran out, the garden would die and so would everyone on board the ship. This was more than a minor malfunction. This was life-threatening.

Taking a deep breath, she tried again. "Explain, *Astrea*."

"System malfunction," the ship repeated, which did nothing but grate on Stella's nerves. Her attention turned upon Eloise, who was the one responsible for the ship's biology functions. She didn't want to believe that a member of her crew could have done this . . . but something had happened. They'd triple-checked the systems when they'd first come aboard. What could have happened since?

Eloise's expression was grim. "I think we need to have an emergency crew meeting."

"It's an outsider job." Jude leaned across the table. "We all know people were pissed about the lotto, about the entire Lifeboat Project. So someone sneaks aboard the ship and disables the system."

"Oh, come on." Leilani pulled a face at the conspiracy theories.

Stella had to admit that Jude had a point—with the final Lifeboat about to leave Earth, there had been chaos. Riots in the streets, shops being looted, buildings destroyed. The lotto's were the system that worked out, but even then people still claimed that it was rigged. There wasn't a quick fix that appeased everyone. It made sense that those left on a dying planet might want to take it out on those who had the chance to leave.

"What?" Jude leaned back, fingers turning his crucifix necklace over and over. "You don't think that one of us would do it, do you?"

Leilani didn't answer, but Warren did, his voice soft and thoughtful.

"Whoever caused the sabotage had inside knowledge of the ship. They picked on something that would take a long time to fix. Something that would be difficult to get done on a limited timeframe. You really want to blame an anti-Lifeboat group for that?"

An uncomfortable silence crept over the table. Eloise wrapped her arms around herself, remaining silent. She looked self-conscious about the event, as she was responsible for the department that had failed. Had Eloise sabotaged the system? She hadn't said anything to defend herself, or anything at all for that matter.

"It has to be a member of the crew," Warren pressed, twisting the knife in the stinging wound of everyone's suspicions.

"Come on, that's bullshit." Arlo shook his head, dark eyes narrowing. "None of us would do that. Not when there's so much at stake."

"Are you willing to bet our lives on that?" Warren asked.

Shivers ran up Stella's spine. She wasn't going to be risking anyone's lives, especially not that of her crew. The idea that someone could be sitting here, knowing that they'd sabotaged the ship and unwilling to speak up . . . it was a dangerous thought. It was like a ticking time bomb waiting to go off. What would that person do, Stella wondered, when their sabotage was exposed?

"It isn't a department fault," Eloise piped up, finding her voice at last. She wrapped her arms even more around herself when she drew everyone's focus. "If it was, I would be able to fix it from the computers there. A system error indicates this is a bigger issue."

"Look, if it's not a fault within the biology department, then it has to be an engineering or mechanical override," Cain interjected. He didn't look at anyone in particular, but there was no doubt where his finger was pointing.

"Seriously?" Leilani scowled at everyone's curious eyes now on her. She pushed herself to her feet. "Alright. If you all seem to think I've done something, I'll go check on the engine room now. Does anyone want to accompany me so I don't fuck anything up on my way down?"

"Leilani . . ." Stella pinched the bridge of her nose at the volatility in Leilani's tone. She felt exhausted, as though she hadn't slept in days. "No one is accusing you of anything. Right now, we're just trying to pinpoint the problem."

Leilani didn't respond, marching out of the room without a backwards glance. They could hear her boots stomping down the corridors as she departed. Stella exhaled, knowing that there was a lot of tension amongst the crew.

"What are we going to do?" Arlo asked, leaning forward in his chair to examine the captain.

"Commence boarding of the lower decks." Stella's shoulders were stiff. "We can't let panic run rife among the passengers. We need to proceed on schedule."

Keeping everything on schedule was what mattered. If they caused unrest among the passengers, *Astrea* would be lost. They had to pretend as though everything was alright. They had enough issues without a potential riot from boarding passengers.

Arlo nodded and began tapping away into the ship's main computer to alert the boarding department to proceed. An uneasy silence descended among the crew. Everyone was suspicious, and the trust that they'd built over their months of training was fraying.

After a few minutes, Leilani returned, a grim expression on her face. Whatever she had discovered in the engine room hadn't been good.

"Leilani?" Stella prompted as the dark-haired engineer swung herself into a chair.

"I couldn't get into the control hub." Leilani folded her arms over her chest. "My access has been revoked."

An uncomfortable silence filled the bridge as they took in Leilani's words. This would mean it couldn't be an outsider job—only another crew member would be able to retract her access. Stella's eyes roved over the others, wondering who the culprit had been. Someone here was lying. Someone here didn't want *Astrea* to leave Earth.

"I'm not flying the ship if we've got a saboteur on board." Arlo shook his head, dark eyes wide with trepidation as his chair swivelled back around so he could face the others. "There are so many things that could go wrong."

"We'll have it fixed, Arlo," Eloise tried to assure him.

"I've got a mum and a sister back down there." Arlo jabbed a finger downwards. His eyes shone and a single tear slipped down his cheek before he wiped it away. "I signed up for this because I thought it would be worth something. If we aren't going anywhere, what's the point? Everything I worked for would be for nothing."

His eyes were wild and his chest heaved with ragged breaths. It looked as though he was hyperventilating. Eloise rested a comforting hand on his shoulder, but Arlo tore away from her, shaking. Stella didn't think she had ever seen him so freaked out. Arlo was always the cool, calm one. He was always there with a ready smile and a crude joke.

"Arlo." Stella raised her hand. "Go to the med bay. Cain, get him something to calm him down, please."

Cain nodded and eased himself up. Arlo followed, his steps slow and uncertain. He was on the verge of panicking, and Stella couldn't afford to let that kind of mindset infect the crew like a disease. Everyone was already tense enough as it was. They didn't need to think about what they were leaving behind, who was still on the ground.

"I don't want to cause alarm," Jude said, clasping his hands together, "But perhaps we've found the person responsible for our current dilemma."

"He's just scared," Stella said, shaking her head. "I don't think Arlo would have sabotaged the mission."

"I agree with Jude." Warren raked a hand through his hair. "I like Arlo. I think he's a great guy. But he's afraid, and sometimes scared people are the ones who do dangerous things."

Stella didn't want to think Arlo could be responsible for something of this nature. She didn't want to believe that whatever had happened to *Astrea* was fuelled by fear. She said nothing, unwilling to condemn Arlo but afraid she could be wrong if she continued to defend him.

Warren headed over to the mainframe computer and started tinkering away. Stella didn't stop him—he was good at his job, and he'd managed to fix all the minor technical glitches they'd experienced so far. This sabotage might be a larger issue, but she believed in his abilities. She believed in everyone's abilities. She just wasn't certain that she trusted their intentions anymore. They didn't have long now until the countdown reached zero, and then the *Astrea* would launch itself to the stars.

"I've managed to restore access to the control hub." Warren declared after about two hours of hard work. The crew had been in various states of unease. Leilani was playing chess with Eloise, a stark contrast to her enthusiastic game with Arlo only a few hours before. How could so much change in such a short space of time? They'd been friends, comrades. Now what were they all?

Stella glanced at Leilani, whose fingers were clasped around her rook.

"Alright. Time to fix this."

"I'll come," Eloise offered, which Stella found odd. Why was she insistent upon accompanying Leilani, when the issue wasn't something Eloise could fix? Stella couldn't help but wonder, in a deep dark part of her, whether Eloise intended to confront Leilani alone. Could she be responsible for what had happened after all?

"I think there's only one person who could revoke access at that level." Leilani's voice was soft, but the implications were clear when she turned her accusatory gaze upon Stella. Her hands were balled into fists, and Stella went cold as the realisation of what Leilani was saying dawned on her.

"Are you kidding me?" Stella demanded, planting her hands on her hips. "Why would I do that?"

"Why would anyone?" Leilani shrugged her shoulders, but her eyes were fierce. "Like I said, you're the only one who has the clearance to do that."

Stella's temper burned like fire through her veins. She couldn't afford to lose control. She couldn't yell at Leilani and tell her that she was wrong, no matter how much she wanted to. The more Stella lost her calm, the more the others might believe Leilani's accusation.

"Just go fix the fucking problem," Stella snapped, refusing to have an argument on the matter.

Leilani's eyes narrowed, but she was a woman of duty, and she marched away with Eloise in tow.

Stella's mind was whirring with possibilities. She couldn't let this ship leave the ground without figuring out who was responsible for the sabotage, but neither could she cause panic by delaying take-off. Leilani would be able to fix the problem—though that was no longer the issue that concerned Stella.

When she looked around the bridge, Jude was sitting at one of the tables in the corner with a bottle of honey-coloured whiskey and a clear glass half-full of it. He wasn't one to drink on the job, but she wasn't about to pass judgement. Right now, everyone was stressed. If alcohol was how Jude chose to cope, that was his business. It didn't stop her commenting.

"You're drinking now?" Stella raised her eyebrows.

Jude's smile was grim. "Just one to ease the nerves."

Stella slipped into the seat across from him.

Jude offered her the glass, and she took a tentative sip. The whiskey burned down her throat like liquid fire. She grimaced, unable to say she liked the taste. She didn't think Jude was drinking it because he thought it tasted good, though.

"Who are you leaving behind?" Stella asked. She'd seen the background checks for the rest of the crew, just as they'd seen hers. Utter transparency—until now, when one of them was hiding a dark secret.

Jude shrugged his shoulders, running a finger around the rim of the glass. "Wife. Kids. My parents, but they're getting old now."

A wave of sympathy cut through Stella for him, despite his matter-of-fact tone. He betrayed no emotion. Either he was good at acting, or he'd detached himself from the idea that he'd have to leave his family behind on Earth. Nonetheless, Jude was not without flaws. He had been one of the first to point fingers when things had gone.

"You've been quick to blame people," Stella said.

He looked up and realised what she was saying. His smile was rueful and sad, as if he was disappointed that she would think to blame him.

"Come on, Captain. What do I know about locking people's access?" Jude shook his head, taking another sip of whiskey.

What do I know about locking people's access? The words caught Stella off-guard. It was true that she was the only one with the clearance to lock people's access. However, there was another person on board with the ability to do it, and she couldn't believe that she hadn't put the pieces of the puzzle together sooner.

"Where's Warren?" She asked, looking around the bridge to find he was no longer there. When Jude looked at her, brows furrowed, she repeated the question with more urgency. "Where's Warren?!"

"Stella!" Leilani's voice, laced with alarm, crackled through her comm. "I need help."

"Leilani?" Stella's fingers fumbled with the comm as she responded. "What's happened?"

"It's Warren." She was crying. Stella's stomach lurched. "It's him, Stella. He's insane. He killed Eloise and I got away from him. I can't go back there. He stabbed me, and . . ."

"Leilani, get to the bridge now. That's an order."

Jude's eyes widened with alarm. He put down his glass and got to his feet. "Should I go and find her?"

"No." Stella shook her head. "If Warren is resorting to attacking people, I want everyone here."

Stella's hands were shaking, her legs trembling as terror rose within her. Whatever she had anticipated, it hadn't been something quite so terrible.

Leilani stumbled in, her hands pressed over her stomach. Eloise's absence was noted. There were tears streaming down Leilani's cheeks, and her fingers were stained red.

Cain launched to his feet and rushed over to her, supporting her as she gripped his arm to keep herself standing upright.

Leilani had gashes across her torso, but nothing that appeared fatal. Nonetheless, there was no way she would be able to fix the malfunction in her condition.

"Cain, get her to medical." Stella raked her fingers through her hair. "Fix her up. Seal yourselves in if you have to."

"Someone needs to fix it." Leilani tried to brush off Cain's arm. "It has to be done."

"I know." Stella took a deep breath. "I'm going to do it."

There was a moment of tense silence as they all realised what that could mean. None of them knew where Warren was. Stella was putting herself at risk to fix the malfunction. There was a loud beeping throughout the bridge, and Stella looked up to see that the countdown was complete. Nausea roiled in her stomach, but she ignored it, forcing herself to focus. Boarding was complete, and it was time to finish what they started.

"Arlo, begin the launch."

"But, Captain . . ."

She fixed him with a firm look, and Arlo knew better than to argue.

He busied himself at the controls as Stella examined the remainder of the crew, wondering if this would be the last time she saw them.

"Once the ship takes off, we are going to need a new technician and a new biologist." She paused, letting the truth sink in. "Maybe even a new captain. There should be those among the civilians with qualifications that fit the bill."

"Stella . . ." Jude murmured, hurt flashing through his eyes at the idea that she might not make it back from this.

She ignored him, turning to face Leilani. "Tell me what I have to do to complete the manual override and get the systems online."

Stella didn't mention to the crew that she had taken the biggest knife from the kitchen when she headed to the control hub. She didn't want any of them to think she intended to kill Warren—but what else was she supposed to do? She didn't want blood on her hands, though she might have no choice.

Outside the control hub, Stella found what she had been dreading, and she pressed a hand over her mouth to stifle a scream. Eloise's blue eyes stared upwards, and there was a blood-red gash carved like a gory smile across her throat. Stella had known Warren murdered Eloise, but it was different to see it for herself.

Stella found it hard to breathe. She kneeled down to close Eloise's eyes, her entire body trembling as panic overwhelmed her. If Warren had managed to ambush the two women, what chance did she have? Taking several deep inhalations to fight off an impending panic attack, she gripped the knife and pushed herself to her feet, entering in the code to access the control hub.

Once inside, Stella followed Leilani's instructions. She didn't rush despite the fact that she was terrified. If she did this wrong, she may as well not have done it at all. When she input the final sequence, the door hissed open and Warren walked in. Stella lurched away from the controls.

"Stella." Warren's eyes were wild, his face stained with blood that wasn't his. "I didn't think it would be you."

"Were you hoping you could finish Leilani off?" Stella's eyes narrowed. The knife was hidden up her sleeve. It pricked her skin, reminding her of its presence. "It's over, Warren. I don't know why you sabotaged the mission, but . . ."

"How do we choose who lives and who dies?" Warren demanded, his voice hoarse and a terrible rawness to his words. "Why are we playing god?"

"We aren't, Warren." Stella's voice shook. If only Warren had expressed his doubts sooner, then this could have ended in something other than violence and death. "We're working with the hand we've been dealt. There was a lotto. It was fair."

"No." Warren's eyes glimmered with unshed tears. "There are billions of people we're leaving on a dying planet. There is *nothing* fair about it."

"So you try and ruin the mission?" Stella asked, her voice breaking. "You killed Eloise. You tried to kill Leilani."

"I didn't want to." Regret flashed across his face. "I didn't want to hurt anyone, but I knew they would find out what I'd done. I thought stopping them would buy me time."

"Where could you go?" Stella walked toward him, one steady foot in front of the other. "There's nowhere to run from what you've done, Warren."

"I know." Warren swallowed hard. "I'm so sorry. I know you won't believe me, but I am."

He lunged at her, but Stella had been anticipating it, waiting for the moment that he would attack. She drove the knife forward, and at the awful sound it made as it pushed into Warren's flesh. Tears blurred her vision, but Stella withdrew the knife and stabbed him again. Once, twice, three times. She had to make sure. She couldn't make the same mistakes that Eloise and Leilani had. Warren couldn't live.

Warren stared down at the crimson stain slowly spreading across his uniform. His eyes were wide and horrified. He hadn't expected her to be here, and he definitely hadn't expected her to kill him. It was Stella's moment of hesitation, born of guilt for what she had done, that turned the tables.

Warren grabbed the blood slick knife from Stella's hand and stabbed her in the chest. It was only once, but it was enough. Stella screamed as pain burned through her, staggering back with the knife still in her. She knew enough from Cain to know what removing it would do—and she had a job to finish. Stumbling over to the controls, Stella's trembling fingers finished the job she had started.

She thought Warren would have wrenched her away or tried to stop her. But stabbing Stella had been his last act—when she whirled around to face her enemy, he was lying on his side, blood dripping down from his multiple stab wounds. His breathing was shallow and his eyes were closed.

Stella collapsed, and the world shuddered around her. *Astrea* was taking off. A faint smile crossed her lips. The agony had stopped and in its place, there was a blissful numbness. As the life bled from her, Stella felt nothing but joy.

We're going to the stars.

About the Author:

Maddie Jensen is a fantasy & science fiction author from Sydney, Australia. She has been reading and writing from a very young age, and is particularly invested in complex characters and well-written female protagonists.

EARTH IN WATER

K.B. Elijah

They laughed at me, before. Told me I was being too pedantic, too picky, too critical. Too worried, too paranoid. Too *me*.

They complained I worked too hard, and demanded I take a break. Was it me for whom they asked such a thing, or themselves?

I heard them imitating me once, or at least I suspected it was me they mocked. A high-pitched and shrill voice that threw my words back to me. Those words whispered things I'd long since tried to block out: *Failure. Stupid. Pointless.*

They lazed around while I slaved under the sun. Every time I thought about joining them, I would be seized by a terror so great that it locked my fingers and froze my tongue. I could not just *sit* there, as they did.

They sighed when I pointed out their errors, and rolled their eyes when I was forced to redo all their work. Could they not understand how important this was?

They did not laugh, afterwards.

They did not laugh when the seas rose to interminable heights, consuming all land but the highest of peaks, when only my ship sailed the flooded earth with none of the holes that they left in theirs.

It was then that I took a break.

About the Author:

K.B. Elijah is a fantasy author living in Brisbane, Australia with her husband and three cockatiels. A lawyer by day, and a writer by . . . also day, because she needs her solid nine hours of sleep per night (not that the cockatiels let her sleep past 6am).

K.B. writes for various international anthologies, and her work features in dozens of collections about the mysterious, the magical and the macabre. Her own books of short fantasy novellas with twists, 'The Empty Sky' and 'Out of the Nowhere' are available in paperback and ebook now. Check out her website at www.kbelijah.com or Instagram @k.b.elijah

The Woman in the Red Bikini

Stephen Herczeg

The great wrought iron gate rumbled back on the embedded track, the small steel wheel squealed as it ran along the metal embedded in the asphalt and paving. Danny cringed as the noise bit through his tired mind and tore to shreds the last vestiges of his consciousness.

As they drove through the darkened streets of the community, Noel, Danny's grandfather, droned on with excessive details about the place. The only words Danny remembered were pool, bowling, mini-golf and gym, the rest ended up in the trashcan of his short-term memory.

The trip from the airport had been quiet. It was late by Perth time, but to Danny's brain, that was still set to Sydney time, it was the middle of the night. Part of him revelled at the thought of staying up until three o'clock, but the reality meant he was unlikely to engage in conversation until rested. Though

Danny knew that never happened. He rarely got more than four hours sleep, and survived on less with a heavy supply of coffee and energy drinks to cope, much to his mother's disgust.

Mum.

As much as Danny loved his mother, he wasn't sure about the current arrangements. She had decided, without consulting him, to ship Danny off to the other side of the country to both spend some time with his grandparents and to give her a well needed break.

Danny knew she just wanted some time to spend with Bill, the newest in a continuous cavalcade of boyfriends. Danny didn't like Bill, and Bill didn't like him. Hence why Danny now rode in a car four thousand kilometres away to spend time with his grandad and nanna, who he hadn't seen for over six years.

They were almost strangers to him, only featuring in scraps of memories from years before. To Danny, the thought of spending the next month with two adults that were half a century older than him was enough to send him over the edge.

Even the cacophony of talk-back radio that assaulted him during the entire journey from the airport made him cringe. Out of some semblance of respect, Danny hadn't put on his headphones like he'd wanted, but he longed for the peace that would come with an ear blasting assault of grind-core metal. The radio had settled into a rare interlude of light classical music. To Danny's ears it actually sounded okay. He'd heard classical music over the years and agreed that some of it was pretty good.

Noel's voice kept a steady murmur over the music, blending into a constant undertone within the overall tune. Danny turned his head and stared out at the darkened houses as they passed by. His bleary eyes caught sight of movement in one of the windows. A scantily clad woman gazed out, appearing as a simple silhouette before disappearing once more. Danny's eyes widened as he made out the shape of her body, highlighted by the light from within. He was both surprised at the vision, and the fact that someone possessing such a figure lived in a place like this.

The curtain dropped back into place, cutting off his view, before he could gain a full appreciation. Danny tried to burn the location into his mind as they drove on. After three more turns, Noel pulled up in front of number 243.

"Here we are, Danny," he said as the garage door trundled up to allow them entry, "your home for the next few weeks."

Struggling to stay awake, Danny glanced across into his grandfather's smiling face and nodded. His silence aimed at keeping a civil tongue.

As they stepped into the house through the connecting door, his attitude was put to the ultimate test as a pair of flabby arms and a cloying aroma of perfume enveloped him.

"Danny, my love," Eileen, his nanna, said, hugging him to her over plump bosom. He almost suffocated in the folds of grandmother and the cloud of smell and only managed to draw breath once she let go of him. He kept up a faux smile as Eileen planted several kisses on his cheeks. "It's been too long; I don't know why we haven't had you over before."

"Too bloody expensive," Noel said from behind. Danny turned to see him lugging a suitcase into the house. Noel pushed past and headed to a doorway halfway down the dim hallway. He pushed the door open and disappeared inside, popping his head out moments later. "This is your room boy."

Eileen unfurled her arms from him. "I've made it up all nice for you," she said, ushering Danny towards his temporary room. They entered and Danny's eyes fell on the queen-sized bed within. He glanced at his phone. It suggested the time was 12:00am. He groaned when he remembered that was 4:00am Sydney time.

"You must be dead tired, how about you get yourself to bed and we can catch up in the morning," Eileen said.

Danny nodded.

Danny's eyes snapped open and saw the sunlight framing the bedroom window with a bright golden glow. Checking his phone, it read five in the morning.

Two hours sleep?

Then he remembered it reset to Perth time just before he fell into bed. Danny groaned again. He'd managed a few hours' sleep, but given his body was still on Eastern time, it felt like eight o'clock, which meant he wasn't going to fall back to sleep until nightfall.

It wasn't just the plane trip that plagued his sleep patterns. His mind kept playing snatches of the conversation he'd overheard. Bill's voice, hushed but insistent, urging his mother to get rid of Danny. His mother agreeing but suggesting they could send him off to Perth for a few weeks.

It was the compliant way his mother quickly agreed that disturbed Danny's mind. He'd always thought they'd been close, but with this new guy in her life, Danny felt that his mother was drawing further away with every passing day.

Danny turned over and tried to sleep, but even as fatigued as he felt he couldn't. It would take a couple of days to adjust to the time difference. After lying with his eyes wide open for a few minutes, he decided to get up and explore. After visiting the bathroom, he padded out to the kitchen and grabbed a glass of water.

His grandparents' house wasn't huge. Within a couple of minutes, he'd seen all there was to see. His bedroom, the lounge, kitchen and his bathroom. All that was left was their bedroom and en suite. Danny grabbed his phone and another glass of water and stepped outside. A blast of early morning heat flowed across his skin, causing sweat to burst out. The shock woke him a little, but as he settled down on the two-seater lounge chair, he became accustomed to it.

As Danny scrolled through his phone, taking an occasional drink to rehydrate his tired mind, he realised his friends were being incredibly quiet on social media. No posts. No messages to him. Nothing of interest. He posted a yearning message with the hope that someone would connect, then locked his phone and stared out across the six-lane road running past the patio. For such a large road, the traffic seemed light for that time of morning, but the speed with which the cars flew past accentuated the noise.

The sliding door opened, dragging Danny out of his musings, and his grandad stepped out onto the patio. Noel wore shorts and a threadbare white singlet, with a few stains down the front. Tufts of grey hair poked through the thin fabric and over the neck.

Noel plonked down next to Danny and murmured a good morning, before putting a cigarette to his lips, lighting it and taking a deep drag. As the nicotine hit Noel's system, he let out a contented sigh.

"I couldn't sleep either," he said, his breath thick with smoke. "That time of year. Too damn hot and sticky." Noel took another drag, leaned his head back and blew out a long stream of white smoke. Out of the corner of his mouth he said, "I'd offer you one, but it's a disgusting habit and I'd have to beat you black and blue if you took it up."

Danny half smiled, unsure if the threat was real, but agreeing with the disgusting aspect of the habit.

Noel remained silent for a while, with the only sound coming from the odd car as it travelled the road before them. Danny sat back, his eyelids drooping under the influence of the intermittent quiet and drone. His eyes snapped open when Noel spoke again.

"I'm sorry you're here boy," he said, "Not the fact you're here, I like you, always have. I'm just pissed at the reason. Your mother shouldn't just fob you off on relatives 'cause she wants to go off and bonk some new bloke."

Shocked at his grandad's candid words, Danny's ears pricked up. "Um, thanks," he said, cautious and curious.

"I'm assuming you don't like this Bill fella," Noel said, glancing over at Danny while taking another drag on his cigarette.

Danny shook his head.

"And I already know he don't like you, or probably just doesn't like kids," Noel continued. "Don't know what your mother sees in him then. Made the same mistake with your Dad." Noel chuckled for a few seconds. "Now there was an asshole, if ever I've met one. Dragged your Mum—with you onboard—across the country, and when you were born hot footed it like the hounds of hell were chasing him. She's never heard from him and never seen any money from him. I told her to come home, but she wasn't having it."

Danny's eyes opened wider. He'd never heard it told like that, never without some form of softening and embellishment. His Mum had always said, she'd and his Dad had grown apart not long after Danny was born, and his Dad had drifted away into a new life.

His grandfather stared at him for a while. "Sorry, didn't mean to be so harsh, but you had to find out one day. I only hope this Bill fella doesn't end up the same way, and I hope he doesn't knock your mother up again. She's still young enough, but hopefully a bit brighter than before."

Noel took another drag on his cigarette and blew a long stream of blue-grey smoke across the patio, before stubbing the butt out in a small ashtray on the table and standing. "Now, I gotta go out for the day. Meeting up with some mates to help one of our friends move house. Got caught putting it to one of the other women in his community. His wife wasn't impressed, so now he's got to leave. Get Nanna to show you around the place. They can get a bit funny here about young kids without adults, but if she introduces you to the guards then you'll be fine to wander around on your own."

Danny watched him leave, his head reeling from the onslaught of information about himself that he hadn't known before. A feeling of sadness washed over him.

Maybe Mum's better off without me?

After fifteen minutes, he wandered back inside, sat down at the table pre-set with breakfast dishes by his grandmother the night before, and drowned his sorrows in coffee, sugary breakfast cereal and a cavalcade of juvenile cartoons on Foxtel.

By the time his nanna wandered out an hour later, Danny had sunk into the well-padded couch after watching too many brain draining cartoons, teetering on, but not able to sleep.

"Danny?" Eileen asked.

He murmured and poked his head up, taking her by surprise.

"Good Lord boy, I didn't see you there," she said, her hand on her chest in shock, "What are you doing?"

"Sorry Nanna, just watching TV."

Eileen looked at the dirty dishes on the table, her face screwed up in annoyance. "You've had breakfast then."

Danny took the hint from the tone of her voice and leapt to his feet. Gathering up the dishes he said, "Sorry about that."

She nodded and stepped out onto the patio to have a cigarette. Danny put the dishes in the sink and slunk off to have a shower.

By the time he returned, Eileen had finished packing the dishwasher and suggested she take him up to the community area to have a look around.

Danny had to slow his stride down to keep his pace level with grandmother's. It wasn't far, but it seemed to take them an age. The day was glorious, looking up into the bright blue sky with a scattering of fluffy clouds on the horizon. The sun bit into his bare arms, the sweat on his back sucking his t-shirt to his skin and damp patches forming beneath his armpits.

They approached a tall, but stocky man in his fifties, and stopped. Eileen introduced Danny to the man. Danny soon forgot his name but didn't forget his job. He served as a Security Guard for the gated community. The man looked Danny up and down, with a hint of suspicion in his gaze. After an uncomfortable minute in which Eileen complained about several things, with the guard keeping his gaze fixed on Danny, they parted, and Danny and his grandmother pushed on towards the community centre.

"Grandad should be home for lunch around twelve thirty, so we've got plenty of time to have a look around," Nanna said.

Walking to the front of the building, Eileen pointed out the swimming pool and gymnasium on their right, and the entrance to the left which led into the main part of the hall. Danny stepped towards the door leading into the hall and entered. In one room was a pool table, and a pair of glass doors let into another room with a wide wooden floor that sat before a raised stage area.

His grandmother was nowhere to be seen. Rushing back to the entrance doors, he stepped out to see her wandering away smoking a cigarette. He called out but just received a wave in response before she disappeared behind a nearby unit.

Danny shrugged and walked towards the pool area. As he reached the door, it opened and a beautiful woman walked out. She had deep brown eyes, with a cascade of dark, wet hair that hung down across her shoulders. She wore a bright red two-piece bathing suit that hugged her ample figure in all the right places.

Danny rarely found older women attractive, preferring to stare at girls in their late teens or early twenties, but this woman ignited something in him. She flicked her eyes towards him and held his gaze as she stepped past, a small smile crossing her lips before she moved on.

He stared at her retreating figure, his hand holding the door open before another older lady stepped up to the opening.

"Shut the bloody door, you young idiot," she said, before grabbing the handle and dragging it shut.

Surprised, Danny simply stared through the glass as the old lady walked away towards the pool. He tried to catch another glimpse of the radiant beauty, but she was gone. Turning back, he checked the location of the old woman, to make sure she was far enough away, before opening the door and stepping through.

Inside the pool area, Danny found several people of his grandparent's age wallowing in the clear water of a ten-metre-long pool. At one end, a pretty girl in her late teens stood and waited for the assembled oldsters to give her their attention. She was dressed in a tight set of gym clothes which showed off her athletic body. When she noticed Danny, she gave him a cheeky smile before tapping her phone to start the music for the oldsters' aqua aerobics session.

Beyond the pool were several pieces of gym equipment including treadmills, exercise bikes, rowers and weight machines. Danny hopped onto the nearest bike and started to peddle until his brow had a sheen of sweat.

He looked up as the entry door opened and a boy, about his age, entered. The new arrival glanced at the oldsters and the pretty instructor before heading across to the gym area. A grin broke across his face as his eyes fell on Danny and he walked over.

"Gidday, I'm Nathan," he said, "Haven't seen you around."

Danny stopped pedalling and replied, "No, just came in last night. Staying with my grandparents."

"Me too. My Dad dumped me on them for the holidays."

"Must be catching," Danny said. "Mum did the same to me, but she wanted to go off with her idiot boyfriend." Danny's eyes fell to the boy's feet. He wore a pair of red, checked old-skool Vans. "Cool shoes."

Nathan looked down and smiled. "Yeah, about the only decent thing my Dad ever got me."

"What's there to get up to around here?"

Nathan smiled, "Around this time of day, I come down here for an hour and pretend to ride one of these bikes."

"Why?"

Nathan's grin grew broader, he tilted his head and nodded towards the instructor. "Why do you think?"

Danny realised what he meant. "Oh, fair enough," he smiled.

Both boys watched the trainer, admiring her form as she jiggled around in time to the music.

"Yep, I think that would be very fair indeed," said Nathan as he mounted the bike next to Danny.

They talked while they pedalled and ogled, comparing their lives and pastimes. Half an hour later, the aerobics session wrapped up and they were left alone.

Bathed in sweat, they stepped off the bikes. Danny panted a little. He hadn't done that much exercise for a while. Nathan took off his shoes, socks and t-shirt, dropped his wallet and a set of keys into his shoe and jumped into the pool. He disappeared under the water and surfaced a moment later. "Well, get your ass in here."

Danny shrugged. "But I didn't bring a towel."

"There's towels in the change room. Besides it's warm enough outside, you'll dry off in no time."

After their swim, they went out to the mini-golf course and played nine holes while their clothes dried off. It wasn't Danny's first time, but Nathan seemed to have the advantage of an extra two weeks with nothing to do. He mentioned he spent time on the course each day and proceeded to wipe the floor with Danny.

As they were putting the clubs and balls away, Danny pulled out his phone and checked the time. It was close to twelve thirty.

"Gotta go, my Nan is expecting me for lunch. You wanna meet up later?" he said.

Nathan said, "Sure."

Danny pulled out his phone. "What's your number?"

Nathan rattled off his phone number and Danny punched it into his own. He pressed the *call* icon.

Nathan's phone played the intro to *Down with the Sickness.*

Danny laughed, "Nice. Old school. Matches your shoes."

Nathan shrugged. "Give you a call later, hey?" he said as Danny moved off.

Danny found the little house abandoned when he returned. A small note on the counter told him that his grandad wouldn't be home, so nanna had gone food shopping.

Great. Didn't need to come home. Oh well.

He fixed himself a sandwich and retired to the patio to watch the traffic and eat. Unconsciously thumbing through his social media feed, he was surprised that none of his friends had posted anything to him.

The evidence from his mother's posts, however, showed her vacation to be the exact opposite of his. Several photos of her and the idiot adorned her page. Danny found one that had her in a joyous mood, something he hadn't seen for years. His finger hovered over the *Like* button until he realised that *he* might be the reason why he never saw her happy.

A sudden wave of sadness washed over him. He shut down the app and turned his phone over to avoid the temptation of seeking further information. Danny sat back and peered out at the ever-present flow of traffic. A tear formed at the edge of his eye. He brushed it away with a finger.

Is this where I end up? Will she actually want me back?

A heavy feeling descended on Danny's chest as the reality of that thought struck home. His thoughts began to sink further, when his phone beeped. Danny turned it over and a smile broke out on his face.

Got something cool to show you. Meet near No. 20. N.

Danny picked his way through the tiny, winding streets of the community, and found the street with a sign indicating houses sixteen to twenty. As Danny walked past the pathway between number eighteen and twenty, he heard a whistle from his left.

Nathan was hiding in the shadows of an overgrown hedge that ran along one side of the path. As Danny joined him in the undergrowth, Nathan nodded towards the back of the houses.

"Follow me," he whispered, putting a finger to his lips. "Be quiet."

They crawled through the bushes, moving past a modest house that looked almost identical to the one owned by Danny's grandparents. The bushes adjacent to the property pushed up against a wire fence that formed the border of the back yard.

Nathan stopped before a small break in the bushes, looked through the wire and into the backyard. He turned, smiled at Danny and pointed, before backing away from the fence and allowing Danny access. Danny crept into the same spot and peeked through the break.

His eyes grew wide at what he beheld.

A woman lay on a sun lounge in the middle of the grassed backyard. The sun streamed down on her naked form, roasting her to a glimmering shade of brown. She was on her stomach, with her face pointed away. Dark hair hung down to the ground. The colour reminded Danny of someone. He searched his memories but was snapped back to reality when she rolled over.

From that moment, Danny only had eyes for her. It was the woman from the gym. Her face said she was much older than Danny, but her toned and athletic body told him he didn't care.

She must do this a lot. There were no lighter areas of skin on her evenly tanned body.

His eyes roved across her torso, taking in her proud breasts that refused to flatten with gravity and her flat stomach that sat just above a neatly trimmed patch of black, curly hair.

"Isn't she gorgeous?" Nathan whispered in his ear, dried leaves crunched under his knees as he manoeuvred himself for a closer look.

Danny nodded. His mind failing to form words as he stared at the sole naked female form he had ever seen in the flesh.

Apart from his mother that is, but he shook that image from his mind and concentrated on the vision before him.

The sound of the mobile phone sitting beneath the sun lounge exploded through the silence. The woman reached down, managing to pick it up and answer without changing position.

"Let's get out of here," Nathan said. "We can come back tomorrow. She's always out here about this time. Unless it's cloudy or wet."

They backed away from the wire and made their way back to the street. Neither saw the woman peer across at the gap in the hedge and smile.

As Danny lay awake that night, a continual stream of images of the naked woman ran through his mind. They stirred something lower down, but fear stopped him doing anything about it. This wasn't his bedroom. Wasn't his house. It was too hard to hide any evidence.

Then Danny remembered he was alone. His grandparents had gone off to a meeting at the communal hall. He smiled in the dark, maybe he could do something. Danny stood up and moved to the doorway, ready to duck down into the bathroom and relieve his tension.

The sound of a key in the lock made him jump back beneath the covers. He lay, wide eyed and wide awake, while his grandparents stomped down the corridor outside.

"Shhh," whispered his grandad. "You'll wake the boy. You walk like a bloody elephant."

"Oh, shut your hole." his nanna said.

They continued on into the lounge room. Danny heard the kettle being filled then the tinkling of crockery as Eileen prepared tea for both of them. Their conversation continued, with the sound of their voices floating through the darkness up the corridor.

Danny crept up to his doorway and listened for a while. Their conversation wasn't important, it only concerned trivia about the complex. Bored, he turned back towards his bed when he heard his nanna say, "What was all that bollocks about the missing boys?"

Danny's ears pricked up and he opened the door a bit wider, straining to hear Noel's reply.

Squeezing through the opening, he crept to the end of the corridor and knelt down to listen.

"What was Vera going on about? She reckons her Sammy just up and disappeared."

Noel replied, "Vera wouldn't know if her arse was on fire. That boy was a weird one. Wouldn't mix with anyone or leave her house for weeks. In the end, he probably just up and went home and he's back with his Mum by now."

"Well what about Enid's grandson?"

"That punk probably got himself arrested or killed by a bikie gang and left in a ditch. I reckon it would have been just a matter of time until someone done him in. Little bastard."

"Well that's not very nice."

"He wasn't very nice. Slouching round the place. Black everything. More metal in his face than in a 60's Kingswood."

"Fine. Should we tell Danny to be careful?"

"He'll be okay. He's knocking around with that other boy, what's his name?"

"Nathan. Staying with Doreen over in Number 124."

"I've seen him around. Seems alright. Doreen's boy always had his head screwed on, I hope the grandson has too."

"If you're sure, but I'm still a bit worried."

"Danny will be fine. Besides, his Mum will have got shot of that bloke by now and he'll be back with her soon."

Danny's heart lifted. He wanted to go home, but part of him didn't believe his grandad. He crept backwards and disappeared into his room.

A slight squeal from his door grabbed Eileen's attention. She stared down the dark corridor before turning away. "You really must oil that door; the breeze must have caught it again."

Danny left the house a little earlier the next day and found Nathan already sitting on an exercise bike. He had a mischievous grin on his face, and Danny soon realised why. He followed Nathan's gaze and saw a bronzed body wearing a red bikini scything through the water swimming laps in the pool.

Danny smiled and mounted the other bike, falling into the same rhythm as Nathan. They both watched as the woman swam from end to end in the little pool and strained for a view every time she executed a tumble turn to change direction.

After several minutes, the door to the gym opened and a parade of oldsters entered. They mingled on the far side of the pool, taking off their gowns to reveal folds of wrinkled skin and flabby flesh.

Danny looked around the pool edge and noticed that the young aerobics instructor was missing, as his eyes caught sight of an old man with sagging man-boobs that hung down from his chest, he shivered in slight disgust. "God I hope I never get that old," he said to Nathan. They both laughed and looked back to the more favourable view.

When the woman noticed the group, she changed direction and swam to the ladder. As she climbed out and stood on the edge, wringing the water out of her long black hair, one of the older women slapped her husband on the shoulder, snapping his attention away from the bikini-clad beauty. The old man turned sheepishly away, much to Danny's amusement.

The woman in the red bikini threw her towel over her shoulder and headed for the doorway. Danny and Nathan's eyes were glued to her behind. She glanced over her shoulder, straight at them. They turned away from her and struggled to find something else to focus on, only looking back as she stepped through the exit.

"Geez she's sexy," Nathan said.

Danny nodded in agreement.

They looked up again as the door opened. Instead of the young girl, an older, matronly woman stepped in, wearing yoga pants and holding a small music system. She stepped up to the edge of the pool and bent over, presenting the boys with the sight of her enormous posterior.

Nathan grimaced and pulled his head back.

"Oh, nasty. Should we get out of here?" he asked. "By now number twenty will be out sunbaking."

"I'm up for that," Danny said with a smile.

They stepped around the aerobics teacher and made a beeline for the exit door. As they stepped outside, a loud crack of thunder rattled across the sky. Above them was a huge bank of dark clouds.

"Crap," said Nathan, flinching as cold drops of rain smacked into his forehead. "My place then?"

"Yeah."

Enjoying his now regular spot on the patio and watching the cars sluice through the heavy rain throwing rooster tails of spray behind them, Danny sipped on his cup of coffee and put it back down next to his empty cereal bowl.

His phone beeped. He snatched it up and smiled as he saw a message from Nathan.

"My plAc. 1 hr. Grs War," it said.

They had played *Gears of War* for almost six hours the day before. Danny's head still reeled, the text message trail they kept up all night hadn't helped either.

The sliding door opened as he put down his phone, followed by the familiar cough, and sound of a cigarette being lit as his grandfather stepped out to join him.

"Morning Danny boy. How are we this fine start to the day," Noel said smiling. He took a long drag on his cigarette then plonked down next to Danny, enveloping him in a cloud of smoke as he breathed out.

Danny suppressed his own cough and managed to choke out, "Okay."

"Have you heard from your mother lately?" Noel asked.

His expression dropped and his mood darkened as Danny realised that his mother hadn't called him since he'd arrived.

"No," he said, his lip dropping a little, "Should I call her?"

Noel patted Danny on the knee. "Sadly, no. I think your Mum's decided to relive her life before you. Can't say I'm happy about it. I've thought about calling her too, but don't want to poke the beast. I can get Nanna to call if you'd like, but she gets upset so easily of late."

The realisation that he might be here a lot longer than he first assumed filled him with sadness. He turned away and stared out at the rain-drenched roadway.

"Sorry lad, didn't mean to bring the mood down," Noel said. "What are you up to today?"

"Nathan's invited me over to play Xbox."

"What's Xbox?"

Danny smiled, "A game console. He brought it with him from Melbourne."

Noel's face showed a mixture of confusion and disinterest.

"We kill things a lot and sometimes race cars, on it."

"Okay, sounds constructive," Noel said.

Danny changed the subject. "Do you know the lady in number twenty?"

His grandfather's face broke out into a wide smile, and his eyes glazed over. "Ah, you've seen Eve, have you?" Noel turned and stared into space, nestling back into the seat cushion and took another deep drag on his cigarette. "Ah, Eve, Eve, Eve. What a beautiful woman!"

Danny nodded in agreement, jumping back in surprise as his grandad sat bolt upright and twisted around.

"Nanna's not about, is she?" he asked.

Noel relaxed when he saw the coast was clear, then bent in close to Danny. The boy had to stop himself recoiling from his grandad's smoky breath. "She moved in about ten years ago."

Danny's eyes widened in surprise as he calculated her age in his head. "She's sixty years old?" he said, adding the mandatory fifty-year age limit to the ten years.

"Supposedly," Noel said, "Incredible isn't it? Hasn't changed a bit in all that time. When she moved in here every bloke suddenly got the hots for her," he chuckled. "Most of them couldn't do anything about it even if they tried." His face went sour, "Including me." Smiling again, Noel continued. "She keeps to herself, does Eve, I've never seen any fellas over there, come to think of it, never seen any visitors either. Strange."

He smiled and glanced at Danny, "Why? Has she caught your eye? You're only young, but I know she's a looker. Way out of your league though, and way too old for you. She'd eat you alive, she would. Stick with the young 'uns." He chuckled to himself and took another drag.

Danny laid his head back on the soft seat cushion and wished he'd never asked.

Later that day, while the rain still pelted down outside, Danny and Nathan hammered each other at Battlefront. Nathan played as the Emperor and managed to corner Danny, as Luke Skywalker, and shock him to death.

"Ah, bugger," Danny cried, "That's the tenth time today."

Nathan laughed and pressed the reset button. As the screen changed, Nathan laid back on the floor and stared at the ceiling. "So, her name is Eve?" he asked.

Danny smiled.

Not this again.

"Grandad reckons she's been here for about ten years. Supposedly, she's sixty years old."

"But, she is so fit. I'd do her without even thinking."

"Like you're really experienced in that area right."

Nathan sat up. "What are you trying to say? You don't think I have?"

Danny smirked and remained silent, watching Nathan's face as his discomfort finally surfaced.

"Oh, okay, you're right, but you've never done it either, have you?"

Danny stayed silent again for a while then laughed. "Course not. Do I look sixteen?"

Nathan sat up, a wide grin on his face. He grabbed the XBOX remote and pressed the *home* button. "Check this out."

He navigated through a few menus, then tapped on one of the icons. The screen changed, bringing up a porn site. Nathan flicked through a few more menus before a video started. On it a young blonde girl engaged with a brawny, well-endowed man in all sorts of sexual acts and positions.

Danny shrugged. "It's porn. I've seen porn before."

"Yeah, but not like this. On your phone or tablet, it's tiny, but this," he threw his hands towards the screen, "Sixty-five inches of solid gold porn. Dad's only got a tiny one at home."

Danny burst out laughing.

Nathan realised what he'd said and joined in. "Hey, I wonder if Eve would be up for something like this?"

"Dude don't be stupid. She's fifty years older than us. She'd only be interested in men."

"I can be a man," Nathan said.

Danny laughed harder and snorted to punctuate it. He was about to make a sarcastic comment when his phone rang. He snatched it up and his face dropped.

"Grandad?" he said, swiping the answer icon.

"Danny mate. Something's happened to Nanna. Get over here now."

The phone went dead before Danny could answer. He grabbed his stuff and rose. "I guess I'll see you tomorrow." he said and rushed from the room.

Danny rushed through the rain. As he rounded the corner into his grandparent's street, he saw red flashing lights ablaze outside their house. He stopped for a second, his mouth open in shock, then pressed on.

As Danny reached the small patch of lawn that served as the front garden, two green-clad paramedics pushed a gurney out of the house. His nanna lay on the gurney, her eyes closed, her face a horrible shade of blue.

"Oh, my God," he blurted out. One of the paramedics looked over at him. Danny was about to ask them what had happened, when his grandad's voice cut him off.

"Danny boy get in here and change into some dry clothes. Be quick. We'll be following the ambulance."

Danny turned towards his grandfather. The sad, sour look on the old man's face stopped any comment. He quickly ducked inside.

The trip to the hospital was quiet. Noel simply maintained his silence. As Danny snuck a glance at him, he looked deep in thought, leaving Danny unsure whether to ask about his nanna's accident. Danny kept silent. He wanted his grandad to open up on his own, rather than get angry from being badgered.

Finally, they could see the Hospital ahead. The ambulance carrying his nanna had cut through the traffic like butter. When they'd lost track of it, Noel had simply headed in the general direction. The paramedics left instructions with Noel to come into the emergency room, then he and Danny would be let straight through.

They found a park near the main entrance. After turning the car off, Noel dropped his head forward onto the steering wheel. "Oh mate, what am I gonna do?" he asked.

Unsure if the question was directed at him, or just at the world as a whole, Danny waited a moment before asking, "What happened?"

His grandfather let out a sigh and turned to face Danny. "She's a bloody fool," he said. "A bloody fool." He sighed again and went quiet for a moment. "She wanted to lose weight. She went on about seeing that bloody Eve the other day. They're the same age supposedly. When you were out, she just wouldn't stop going on and on about how slim Eve was and how fat she was. I told her I don't care. I love your Nanna just the way she is, but she still went up there this morning. To the pool. To join those other idiots in that aerobics class. Red as a bloody beetroot she was when she got back. I made her a cup of tea and put her in her favourite chair. I wasn't gone a minute and when I came back she was asleep, but she didn't look right. I checked, she wasn't breathing, then I think I freaked out. I've watched those videos on the telly. I dragged her off her chair and onto her back and thumped her chest. I did that CPR thing, breathing into her mouth, and thumping her chest. Finally, she coughed and started breathing again, but she wouldn't wake up. That's when I rang the ambulance."

Noel turned back and dropped his head on his hands. Danny could hear the sobs cutting through his voice.

"I just hope she's okay," he said. "I don't know what I would do without her."

They sat in silence for a while.

Once he'd composed himself, Noel stepped out of the car and headed towards the hospital. Danny fell in time with his grandad's rhythm. They made their way through the emergency room and, after speaking to a nurse on the front desk, were taken into a small ward. There Eileen lay still on a bed, an oxygen canula affixed to her nose.

Danny's heart sank. She looked so small on the bed and her skin still had a strange tinge of blue to it. From the crime shows he watched on the telly, he knew that shade meant that she had been starved of oxygen. He also knew that anyone who went without oxygen for a long period of time may suffer brain damage. His heart sank deeper.

A Doctor entered the room to check his nanna's chart. Noel, sitting nearby, cleared his throat and indicated for Danny to come and sit next to him.

"Try and ring your mother, if you can, tell her what's happened," he said, trying to coax a smile onto his face, but it just looked like he was in pain.

Grandad's downcast eyes betrayed his inner worry. Standing, Danny nodded and moved away to another seat, leaving his grandfather alone. He pulled out his phone, mindful to keep an ear out for any information, and tapped in his mother's number, but as expected was greeted by her cheery voice telling him to leave a message. He waited for the beep before saying, "Mum, it's me. Something's happened to Nanna. She's in the hospital. Grandad wanted me to call. Please ring back." Staying silent for a moment, Danny searched for more to say, but before he could, the message recorder cut out. He stared at his phone for a moment, cursing his mother under his breath, before putting the phone back in his pocket.

Another doctor ducked inside the curtain, and Danny strained to listen in, but only caught snatches of the conversation. Words and phrases such as, "Serious stroke, coronary damage, oxygen starvation," and "possible cerebral damage," drove his mood even deeper.

He sat down next to his grandad. After staring at the ceiling for a few moments, he was lulled as he listened to the sounds of the emergency room carrying on around them. Time swept by in a daze of unrelenting action while Danny sat cocooned in a shell of nothingness.

At some stage, his grandad disappeared before coming back reeking of cigarette smoke. He sat by Danny for few moments before moving to his wife's bedside.

Danny closed his eyes, enjoying the darkness it brought, only to open them in dismay. He felt like he'd fallen into a disturbed sleep only to be snapped out by movement nearby. When Danny checked his phone, he was shocked to see that two hours had passed and there was still no reply from his mother.

He noticed movement behind the curtain of his nanna's bed.

Noel emerged, his shoulders slumped. "It's not good boy, not good at all," Noel said, dropping his head into his hands and breathing deep sighs. "They'll be moving her to intensive care. I'll take you home. Boys your age shouldn't have to sit around this sort of place. Too many sick and dying people. It's not good for you." His voice dropped to a mumble. "Not good for me neither."

An orderly pulled back the curtains and guided the gurney as a second one pushed it. Danny and his grandad watched as the shrunken form of the once formidable woman wheeled past them.

A doctor stepped over to Noel. "We'll take her up to the ICU now. We can only have one visitor at a time." He dropped his eyes to Danny, "but there's a visitor lounge that you are welcome to use."

"It's okay, I'll take the boy home. No use him sticking around here until something changes," Noel said.

The doctor patted Noel on the shoulder and nodded, before striding after the gurney.

Noel stood up, mimicked the doctor and patted Danny on the shoulder. "Okay boy let's make tracks. Did you get on to your Mum?"

Danny shook his head, "No. I left a message, but she didn't answer."

His grandad's face looked grim. "Try again later for me, or at least in the morning."

Danny nodded.

Danny's eyes fluttered open. As usual, sunlight streamed into the room around the edge of his blinds. It didn't mean much; it could still be as early as five in the morning. Perth's lack of daylight savings was still a mystery to his Eastern state honed mind.

He rolled onto his back and stared at the ceiling. The whirlwind of activity and emotions of the last twelve hours churned through his mind.

It was dark by the time his grandad dropped him home. They'd stopped by a greasy fast food joint on the way and picked up something to eat. From his attitude, it wasn't something Noel ate a lot, preferring the food prepared by Eileen. They'd eaten in virtual silence, caused mostly by Noel's morose mood.

It wasn't aimed at him, Danny knew that, it was a combination of fear and anger brewing inside his grandfather's mind. Noel had confessed that he always thought he'd be the first to go. Danny tried to reinforce the idea that Eileen was alive and would make a full recovery. His grandad scoffed at the suggestion.

Danny found it a relief when Noel left for the hospital, leaving half his burger uneaten. Danny cleared up the dishes, had a shower and spent the rest of the night ignoring a cavalcade of mindless TV shows before crashing into bed.

From nearby, his phone beeped, dragging him from his remembrance. Danny snatched it up, hoping it was his mother returning his messages. His heart dropped as he found it was a message from his dentist reminding him of an appointment in two days time.

Great another thing to remember. Cancel the stupid appointment.

Danny dropped the phone back on the side table and stared at the ceiling. He was only fourteen, far too young for this sort of crap. It was school holidays. He should be out doing stupid things with his friends, or wasting his time watching TV or playing video games, not worrying about his family and his future.

Danny snatched up his phone again and checked the messages. Nothing. He scrolled social media to see if his mother had posted anything. Again nothing.

She's posted every other day, why not today?

Danny thought about ringing again, but just dropped the phone back down. What he needed was a shower and strong coffee.

Sitting on the patio, with an empty cereal bowl and steaming cup of coffee resting nearby, Danny glanced at his phone. It may have been the constant somnambulistic hum of traffic as it passed by, or the deluge of thoughts and feelings from last night's events assaulting his subconscious, but the urge to check his social media feed has faded.

Reaching for his coffee, Danny's hand bumped his phone and set its screen alight. He stared at the icons. No new messages. Nathan hadn't replied to the call to arms he'd sent out earlier. No new social media posts. His friends back East seemed to have all but forgotten about him.

Just like Mum.

The absence of message replies also meant that his mother was missing in action. Danny shook internally, imagining what that action could be. He gazed at a gun metal grey mustang as it swept past, its deep throated V8 engine gurgling and roaring as the driver stabbed at the accelerator.

Danny sipped his coffee, put the cup down and dropped his head back on the seat cushion. Questions pummelled his mind. Questions about his future. About his mother. About his grandparents.

What the hell do I do now?

He was young. He wasn't meant to have worries. That was the world of adults. He'd heard the stories about teenagers having to suddenly step up and become adults almost overnight. Not something Danny ever wanted to embrace or even think about, but with his nanna's collapse, it might be thrust on him instead. His mind clicked up a gear, gunning his internal accelerator and starting an argument.

I'll just go back East.

Why? What's really there for you? A mother that doesn't want you around. Friends that don't seem to care.

It's where I belong?

That's a cop out. You're just neglecting your duty.

What would you do?

Maybe seek out those that actually love you. Your grandad has been nothing but kind and loving since you got here. He's gonna need help if your nanna dies. Besides . . .

Danny opened his eyes and stared out across the pattern of beige and cream houses, topped red and orange roofs. Their green front lawns resplendent in the bright sunshine. The towering trees highlighting the idyllic nature of the image.

It's nice here. The people may be a little behind the times and suffer from a touch of narrow mindedness, but they are generally nice.

You could be right.

And you've made a friend. He at least likes you, a bit different to the losers you hang around with back East.

Hey, those are my friends.

Are they? Are they really?

Danny thought for a moment. He'd argued with himself and lost. The trouble lay in the fact that he felt he needed to lose.

You're right. I'll think about it. See how things pan out over the next few days. I'll at least stay and help Grandad until Nanna comes home. If she comes home.

Good. I'm glad we could have this little chat. I'm always here if you need.

The logical part of his mind went silent. Danny grabbed his coffee and downed it in one steaming gulp. He winced as it burnt his tongue but was grateful for the caffeine hit that would come.

He checked his phone and sent an instant message to Nathan. Staring at it for a couple of minutes, he became fed up with the lack of a reply. It was time to pay a visit to his new friend.

Danny walked through the community and glanced up at the sky. A blanket of crystal-clear blue greeted him, the clouds of the last couple of days all but gone, with only a couple of small fluffy balls gripping the far-off horizon.

Danny checked his watch and smiled. The aerobics session would be starting in a few minutes. He pondered heading for the community centre instead but shook his head and walked on towards Nathan's place.

As he was about to knock on the door, the familiar sound of garden shears *snicking* together, as they lopped off some of the overgrown foliage on a well-manicured hedge, floated across. Danny turned and saw a floppy and faded red hat bobbing up and down behind the thick bushes. He was familiar with that hat and its owner Mr. Rodgers.

Danny grabbed the door knocker, rapped three times and waited. A voice came from the other side of the hedge. "They ain't home, you know."

Danny turned and found the face of Mr. Rodgers staring over the hedge at him. "Brown's gone off. I saw the silly bugger heading for the pub yesterday lunch time. He ain't been back. Probably got himself arrested again. Doreen went out earlier, assume she's looking for him."

"Have you seen Nathan? Their grandson?" Danny asked.

Mr. Rodgers thought for a moment, his face creasing up with the effort. "No. Not since late yesterday. Thought he must have gone off to look for the old man as well. Hope he's okay. Seems like a nice kid. Don't know what's wrong with Brown's son. Dumping the kid on his parents. Disgusting it is."

"Thank you," said Danny, trying to break Mr. Rodgers's train of thought and any accompanying monologue.

Mr. Rodgers stopped for a moment, then said, "No worries then," and went back to his gardening.

Danny walked away and with no real idea of where to look, headed for the community centre, the first place that Nathan and he had met.

His timing was correct. The aerobics session had begun. The older woman led the session, taking the oldsters through their routines. Danny glanced across at the exercise bikes. All were empty. He thought about asking around if anyone had seen Nathan, but the question of why would they care or know came to mind, so he left.

Confused, Danny started to wander around the complex, searching for something, but not sure of what or even why. He pulled out his phone again and checked the messages. Nothing. Tapping the social media icon and scanning through the posts and messages revealed the same. Nathan hadn't posted anything all day. He hadn't even looked at the earlier message Danny had sent him.

Then Danny's eyes fell on the message he'd sent his mother. It indicated that she'd seen it over an hour before. That's all. Nothing more. No answer. No phone call. No text message.

Disappointed, he brought up her number and phoned. The machine answered again. "Mum," he started, "It's Danny. Where are you? Why won't you ring? Why won't you text? Nanna's in hospital. She might die. Don't you care?"

When the machine beeped and cut him off, Danny stared at the screen for a few moments. Tears welled in the corner of his eyes. The screen of the phone remained impassive.

Danny felt a welling pit of despair building in his soul. He needed Nathan, or at least someone to talk to, otherwise he would be sucked down into the black void.

He brought up Nathan's number and hit *dial*. Half expecting to be rejected once more, he waited for the answering machine message. As the phone tone changed to long beeps as the connection established, he played Nathan's ring tone in his head. It took him a moment to realise it wasn't in his head.

Danny pulled the phone away from his ear and listened. There it was. The song played nearby. He concentrated on the direction, but the answering machine cut in. Danny rang again and listened. When the song started up, he looked in the direction of the music and realisation dawned. He stood outside number eighteen.

You bugger. You're perving on Eve and ignoring me.

Danny put his phone away and clamoured through the underbrush towards the opening they had used to view the wonderful sights on display.

The clearing was empty. No Nathan. Danny turned and checked the backyard. No Eve. Confused, he sat on the dry carpet of leaves and sticks. He pulled his phone out again and as his finger was poised over the call button, he spied a phone lying in the underbrush nearby.

Danny snatched it up and looked it over. It seemed familiar. His finger brushed the screen and a lock image popped up, showing a photo that he and Nathan had taken a couple of days ago. That solved that problem. Nathan had been here but had dropped his phone.

Was he scared off? Dragged away?

Danny checked the ground. There were no scuff or scrape marks. It all seemed as neat and tidy as a small patch of nature could be.

No closer to finding his friend, he crawled back out to the street and examined Nathan's phone. He tried to remember the lock combination, but after three failed attempts gave up and put it in his pocket.

A soft lilting voice floated towards Danny, snapping his attention to the source.

"Danny? Isn't it?" the voice said.

Danny saw the owner and his eyes almost fell out of his head. Before him stood Eve, the wondrous owner of the red bikini, looking at him. Instead of the bikini, she wore a loose, flowing bathrobe. Danny tried to stop staring, but his imagination went into overdrive trying to picture what was underneath.

"You look lost," she said, "Can I help?"

Danny snapped out of his fantasy and said, "My friend. I think he was here."

She smiled, "Would that be Nathan?"

He nodded.

"I saw him yesterday, but he hasn't been around today." She waved a hand in front of her face. "It's already getting hot. You look thirsty. Would you like to come in for a drink?"

Danny found himself nodding. Something about this woman, apart from the obvious allurement of her beauty, even her voice was attractive, in a soporific way. Danny found himself drifting on her words and was surprised when he followed her inside. All the lessons of childhood regarding strangers were washed away on the ripples of her charm.

As he entered, Danny took in the details of Eve's house. Compared to his grandparent's house it was a temple to Marie Kondo. Each room contained the bare minimum of furniture to make it liveable and almost every horizontal surface was uncluttered without a single vase or knick-knack to be seen.

"You have a nice house," Danny stammered, words always failed when he was near a woman he found attractive. Eve glanced around, as if seeing the rooms nearby for the first time. She turned her head back to face Danny.

"Thank you," she said smiling and pushing past to head down the hallway.

Danny followed and found the corridor opened up into a kitchen area. Eve moved to the fridge and withdrew a bottle of cola and a chilled glass.

"Is this alright?" she asked, pouring him a drink before he could respond.

As Danny took it from her, he noticed her robe open, taunting him with a covert glimpse of what lay beneath.

"Do you like what you see?" she asked.

Danny choked on a mouthful of cola, spritzing it up and out through his nostrils. He slammed the glass down on the counter, almost knocking it over as he fought the sensation of liquid being dragged down his trachea.

Danny wretched and coughed, dislodging the cola from his windpipe and regaining control of himself.

Eve stood wiping the counter with a cloth and watching Danny with intent.

Danny stared at his hands, they were covered with sticky residue and he could feel it all over his face. "Can I use the bathroom to clean myself up?"

"Sure, down the hallway, first on the right, through the bedroom," she said, a small smile on her face.

Danny raced off and found the bathroom. He washed his hands and face, then took the opportunity and relieved himself. As he washed his hands for the second time, he stared at himself in the mirror.

What the hell are you doing here?

If all goes well boyo, living the dream.

Don't be stupid. She's old enough to be my nanna.

But she looks younger than your mum.

Shut up.

Danny stopped the voices and stared at his face for a few moments. He needed to get out of there. It wasn't right. Nothing was right about this.

As he turned and stepped into the bedroom, it occurred to him that this must be Eve's bedroom. Danny stopped and looked around. Again, the room was a simple affair, with only a small bed in one corner and a walk-in wardrobe next to the bathroom.

A flash of red caught his eye on the floor of the wardrobe. With thoughts of the bikini racing through his mind, Danny ignored his better judgement and stepped towards the closet to check. Rather than turn on the light, he pulled his phone out and flicked on the torch. As he brought the light around, he saw that, instead of Eve's bikini, it was a pair of red checked old-skool vans sneakers.

His mouth dropped open in realisation.

Nathan's shoes. How the hell did they get there?

Suddenly, the bedroom light flicked on. Danny turned and found Eve standing in the doorway. A small smile played across her lips as she looked at him.

"You were an awful long time, I wanted to check that you were alright," she said.

Danny looked at her, then back at the shoes. "Nathan's shoes? How?" he asked.

"I told you I saw Nathan yesterday. He must have left those behind." She stepped into the room. "He wasn't the same by the time we finished." She dropped a hand to the belt of her robe and, drawing her hand away, the robe parted. She shrugged and let the robe slip from her shoulders and pile on the floor.

Danny was awestruck. Before him was a naked goddess. Her firm breasts stood high and proud, her flat stomach taught and toned, showing the relief of the muscles beneath. He tried to drag his eyes away, his mind thrashing on his internal thoughts.

She's as old as Nanna. Stop looking. This is so wrong.

Reading his mind, Eve smiled and stepped forward until her fragrance washed over him. Danny had never been into perfume, but whatever Eve wore sent tendrils of fascination through his mind. She reached out and grabbed his hands. Danny succumbed and dropped his phone. It bounced on the carpet and landed a metre away, the lock screen facing the ceiling.

Eve brought Danny's hands up to her breasts, giving the teenager his first ever feel of the female form. She leaned in and whispered into his ear. "Doesn't that feel wonderful?" she said as she wrapped her arms around Danny and pulled him closer.

Danny could hardly breathe. His body felt like jelly, except for the stiffening feel within his shorts. He was on the verge of passing out, part from fear, part from excitement.

Eve pushed into his hands. Danny felt the nipples grow hard and ran his fingers across them.

She groaned. "Ah, that's good. You're gentle. Good. Much better than Nathan. He was too rough."

At the mention of his friend's name, Danny drew back in horror. "Nathan?"

Eve smiled. "Don't worry about him. He can't bother us now."

Danny tried to drag himself away, but the gentle feeling of delirium washed over him again. His mind felt like he wanted to run, to get away, but his body wouldn't let him.

He gaped back at Eve and noticed her face had changed. Her eyes were now yellow instead of blue. The pupils were elongated and thin. Her breasts felt strange as well. He dropped his gaze, pulling his hands back at the same time. Her breasts were gone, the skin seemed old and cracked. Flaking or made of scales. He looked back at her face. Her nose became two elongated slits. Her mouth stretched out across her entire face, her tongue flicking in and out was long, thin and forked at the end.

He grimaced as she tightened her grip. It was uncomfortable, constricted, pain shot up and down his back. He glared down in horror. Eve had no arms, she was now just a long thin body, covered in small, green scales, wrapping around him several times.

Danny stared back at Eve's face. The transformation was complete. The face of the beautiful woman was gone, replaced by the malevolent visage of a massive snake.

She opened her mouth, baring her long, wicked fangs and hissed at him, "You boys. So young. So virginal. So delicious. So full of the life essence that keeps me young. Has kept me young for millennia."

Danny fought in vain against her hold. Her elongated body held his arms jammed against his sides. The snake woman reared up, picking Danny off the floor, slowly squeezing the air from his lungs, slowly crushing the life from him.

As dark spots formed before his eyes, Danny dropped his head and spied his phone. The screen lit up as it received an incoming call.

Danny's failing mind concentrated on the screen, trying to read the name of the caller. It was a name he'd been longing to see for days.

Mum?

About the Author:

Stephen is an IT Geek, writer, actor, film maker and Taekwondo Black Belt based in Canberra Australia. He has been writing for over twenty years and has completed a couple of dodgy novels, sixteen feature length screenplays and dozens of short stories and scripts.

Stephen's scripts TITAN, Dark are the Woods, Control *and* Death Spores *have found success in international screenwriting competitions with a win, two runner-up and two top ten finishes.*
His horror stories have featured in various anthologies including: Sproutlings; Hells Bells; Trickster's Treats #1, #2 and #3; Shades of Santa; Below the Stairs; Behind the Mask; Beyond the Infinite; Beside the Seaside; The Body Horror Book; Anemone Enemy; Petrified Punks; Beginnings; Sea of Secrets, Demonic Carnival; Deep Space; A Tribute to H.G. Wells; What If?; Through Death's Door *and* Coffins and Dragons.

Over forty of his drabbles have been accepted by Blood Song Books; Black Hare Press; Fantasia Divinity and ThingsInTheWell.

Several of his Sherlock Holmes pastiches have been accepted for inclusion in anthologies published by Belanger Books and MX Publishing.

You can catch Stephen at his Facebook page:
https://www.facebook.com/stephenherczegauthor

This Is the Dawning (Part IX)

Helena McAuley

His father had named him Elham—a beautiful inspiration. The name was supposed to reflect the love his father had felt for the third-born son, and his joy at his birth. But even in youth, the name came to reflect the character of the child. Drawn to anything and everything beautiful—vibrant flowers, sensual cloth, delicate pottery, ghazal and Safavid poetry—the young Elham also inspired beauty wherever he went. As the boy became a young man, his father's pride turned first to suspicion, and then chagrin, as his son and refused to leave beauty behind.

On the eve of his twenty-sixth birthday, Elham was supposed to be a good son and come home to discuss marriage proposals, as his older brother and sister had done. His delicate features and soulful dark eyes already caused the young women to swoon. He would be replete with offers. Elham came, wearing the ridiculous silver in his hair that had been his custom for the past few years. His father was sure it was painted on but had never caught the young man in the act. Yes, he came. But the father did not get what he wanted.

"No, Baba," the young man had said with a kind smile. "I will not marry."

His father's fears had been confirmed. "You do not love women."

"I love *all* women," he had responded. "Just as I love all men. But I do not love their flesh. I love their hearts. I cannot commit to one person, because I could never remove my love from all others. Any wife I would take would divorce me for my lack of action."

His father's face turned to contempt. "Then you find your love in the arms of *men?*"

Elham shook his head. "You do not understand. I cannot find love in the arms of *anyone*. I do not have the desires of men, and it would be an injury to any woman who would take me as a husband. I love, Babayı, but I will never be known by another person."

He took his father's hand, his dark eyes and kind smile filled with sorrow. "I cannot remain in your house. Babayı . . . *Let me go.*"

And he did. As if he were powerless to even think otherwise.

All Elham took with him were the clothes on his back, and the name his father had given him. Elham—*a beautiful inspiration.* It was the one thing he could not part with.

Leo had been waiting for him in the falling twilight. Elham crushed himself into the massive man and wept openly on his chest.

"There, there, Virgo," Leo had said. "You've done the right thing."

His words were marred with tears. "I love my family."

"I know."

"But I do not belong with them!"

"I know."

Leo had incarnated decades before, and Elham knew his fellow understood his pain. Elham allowed himself to weep until it was leeched from him. Then he dried his eyes and began a new life.

The Spirit of Virgo, incarnate in the form of Elham, travelled the world. As part of a select crew that Leo—the famed tenor *Leonardo Cantari*—refused to perform without, he had inspired poets and composers, set designers and costumers. He had also inspired women into Leo's arms. He brought *joy*

and *love* to every performance, and, in turn, he derived joy and love from every moment.

In the subterranean catacombs of Her Majesty's Performing Arts Centre, surrounded by racks of costumes, he was expressing that love right now.

"I love *glitter!* So much *glitter!* I love *diamonds*, and *sequins*, and *bling!*" As he sang, he tossed a bejewelled scarf around the neck of a costumed mannequin and gave it a critical look. They were only performing a selection of arias—a marketing event to promote the opening of the operatic season—but Elham saw no reason that the costumes should be less than perfection.

Leo's voice sang inside his mind; *Elham, Capricorn and 'Douglas' are on their way to you.*

Elham sent back an acknowledgement, his long, deft fingers finding a stray thread. Throughout many incarnations, he and Leo had been drawn to one another; a bond greater than fidelity, a bond greater than even love. Like the mistletoe that clings to the oak tree, Leo's indomitability offered Virgo shelter, and Virgo's capricious love brought softness to Leo's hard edges. Their near-symbiotic companionship had become a mainstay of both their existences, to the point that, once incarnate, neither could fathom existence without the other.

Elham wound the thread around his finger until it was taut, and then reached out for the heavy sewing scissors. So

Aquarius—Douglas—was finally here. The trill of nervous excitement that coiled in his stomach nearly unsettled his hands, and it was almost more than he could manage to keep himself attuned to his task. His hands groped for the scissors on the table next to him until he was forced to turn his head.

They were gone. But he'd left them right there . . .

"There's a lovely weight to these," an unfamiliar voice said from behind him. "Grounding. Reassuring, even."

He turned, the thread pulling from the scarf as he did, and beheld a girl of maybe fifteen or sixteen, twirling the scissors in her small hands. Dark eyes lit with fire were fixed on him, and there was a dangerous edge to her smile.

"Hello, Virgo."

"Aries!" he said with a start as recognition came to him. "Well, look at you! *This* is a new look. Very different since the last time I saw you—when was that again?"

"The Storming of the Bastille."

Elham cringed. "Oh, yes," he said. "You enjoyed yourself, that day."

The mirthless smile grew. "Yes. I did."

Elham repressed a shudder at the memories of blood and death. He held out his hand. "May I have my scissors, please?"

"Where would you like them?"

It was the edge to her voice, more than the words expressed, that caused him to pause. He again took in her casual stance, her grip on the tool-turned-weapon. In the hands of Aries, anything could become a weapon. His throat turned dry. The distance between them seemed too small.

"I have already declared for Aquarius," Elham said in a small voice.

"I know."

"Killing me here won't sway anyone," he said. "It will only strengthen their resolve."

"I know."

She moved, not unmanifest, but still faster than Elham could comprehend. Her unencumbered hand grasped his throat and lifted him from his feet. He was taller than her, but her slight form was unbowed by the action. From the corner of his eye the blade of the scissors caught the light and gleamed.

"Virgo," she said. "How well can you control your physical form?"

The air could not escape his throat to form words, so he resorted to a more fundamental form of speech. *But it's not yet the Dawning!*

True, Aries replied. "Sagittarius would prefer I sway you," she continued, returning to verbal speech. "Our side is one down, after all. But some of us have a better idea." She drew him closer to her face, though he still never touched the ground. "Some of us *want* the battle," she purred.

He had been prepared to unmanifest and escape her grasp, but her words sent his blood cold.

Scorpio.

Aries grinned. "And myself."

You're not one down! Elham pleaded. *Taurus—*

"Is dead," Aries responded. Her hand rose, and with it the shining blade.

Elham clutched at the hand about his throat, legs kicking frantically as he struggled in her grasp. *Libra!* he screamed. *There's still Libra!*

The hand stilled.

Fear churned in Elham's bowels as he watched the blade.

Aries looked away from him, as if listening to some internal voice—as if listening to an external voice made internal.

"Libra would do," she mused, and threw Elham.

He crashed against the sewing table, knocking the heavy machine to the floor and grasping at his burning throat. Air leaked through his crushed windpipe with a horrid wheeze. With great effort he swallowed, wincing at the lump that passed, and then forced his physical body to mitigate the damage, the soft tissue creaking and expanding into its familiar form.

When he looked up, Aries was smiling at him.

"*You* will find Libra for us," she said.

Elham started. "*Me?*" Despite his reconstructed windpipe, the noise still came out as a squeak. "I don't know where Libra is!"

"Capricorn does."

Elham's heart stilled inside his chest. That was true. Capricorn would know where Libra was. Capricorn would *always* know the whereabouts of Libra. Not only because he had made it his mission to know the movements of all of the Twelve, but for more personal reasons. Would Capricorn see this as an act of betrayal? Was it? To betray the most insular of the Twelve into the hands of Aries? Of Sagittarius?

Of Scorpio?

Bent and slumped against the table, Elham trembled with indecision. His life, or the life of one of his fellows? How much was one life worth?

He reached out . . .

Aries' fist flew into his face.

"Not a *word* to Leo," she growled.

But Leo had already felt the connection, was reaching back with an enquiring mind; searching him, questioning him. Elham's face tightened as he sent out waves of reassurance.

"Not a word," he whispered to Aries, and his heart broke.

Despite her slight form, Aries towered over Elham's crumpled form. "Deliver Libra to us." Her voice was soft, but it was a softness surrounded by flames. "Or we will take you instead." She grinned at him, and her dark eyes trailed across him. "Such a pretty incarnation," she drawled. "Shame to destroy it. But you would be no contest in battle, anyway. At least your destruction would serve purpose."

She righted herself and, with only a passing glance, unmanifest.

Despite his limited mastery over his incarnate form, Elham could not slow the hammering of his heart. With trembling hands, he gripped the table and forced himself to stand. He looked about the room. "Aries?" She was gone, but a presence still remained.

"Aries?" he pleaded again. He realised the room was too small, the racks of props and costumes offering too much concealment. His breath became trapped in his chest. The coat hangers swayed and knocked against each other.

"Aries! Stop it!" he cried, retreating to the centre of the room and the feeble security of distance it offered. The walls closed around him, fear mooring his feet as if in mud and sand.

Shadows moved.

"Scorpio?" he breathed.

The door behind him crashed open, and Elham's heart seized with terror. He spun, every muscle tensing, fearing what he would see but unable to stop himself from facing it. He met stern, grey eyes, and he almost sagged with relief.

"Capricorn! What a lovely surprise!" The relief that washed his face was not contrived—not even Scorpio would outright attack him, now. But the joy in the smile he wore was feigned. He may be safe, but he was not delivered; not yet.

Likewise, he could not keep at bay the shaking of his hands as he took that of the boy who stood by Capricorn's side. A wimp of a thing, not what he would have expected from Aquarius.

"A pleasure to meet you, Douglas," he said. "I am Virgo."

In the privacy of his own thoughts, he could not help but add; *And I am about to betray you.*

To be continued in the next edition of the Zodiac Series— *Libra* . . .

About the Author:

Helena McAuley has been called an 'idealist', a 'dreamer', and a 'fantasist'. She has also been called many other things that cannot be reprinted in a polite anthology.

When not being likened to gorgons, harpies, or mythical canines, Helena likes to read about these, and many other things. Preferably on a sunny day, while sitting under a tree, wearing SPF-1,000 and sipping on a well-chilled beverage that may or may not be alcoholic.

'This is the Dawning' is a serialised debut that will be published throughout the ASF Zodiac series. Virgo looking to betray Cap and Doug? This can only end in trouble for someone! Read on to find out who.

Helena can be found (mostly) twit-ing, (sometimes) insta-ing, and is (rarely) facebookified under the handle @thathmc

ABOUT AUSSIE SPECULATIVE FICTION

Aussie Speculative Fiction is a recently established group which was created to support and promote Australian speculative fiction writers.

Check out our links:

www.facebook.com/Aussiespeculativefiction/

www.twitter.com/aussiefiction

www.aussiespeculativefiction.com

www.books2read.com/rl/asf

ABOUT DEADSET PRESS

Deadset Press is the publishing imprint of Aussie Speculative Fiction—a community aimed at supporting Australian and Kiwi authors. You can learn more at:

www.aussiespeculativefiction.com

ALSO BY DEADSET PRESS

<u>Annual Anthologies</u>

Beginnings: Aussie Speculative Fiction Anthology Vol. 1

Journeys: Aussie Speculative Fiction Anthology Vol. 2

\#

<u>Drowned Earth</u>

Prequel: Shards of Silver by Alanah Andrews

The Rise by Sue-Ellen Pashley

Fire Over Troubled Water by Nick Marone

Submerged City by Austin P. Sheehan

Tides of War by Marcus Turner

The Jindabyne Secret by Jo Hart

River of Diamonds by S. M. Isaac

Salvaged by C.A. Clark

Emoto's Promise by Shel Calopa

\#

<u>The Zodiac Series</u>

Capricorn (The Zodiac Series #1)

Aquarius (The Zodiac Series #2)

Pisces (The Zodiac Series #3)

Aries (The Zodiac Series #4)

Taurus (The Zodiac Series #5)

Gemini (The Zodiac Series #6)

Cancer (The Zodiac Series #7)

Leo (The Zodiac Series #8)

Virgo (The Zodiac Series #9)

Libra (The Zodiac Series #10)

Scorpio (The Zodiac Series #11)

Sagittarius (The Zodiac Series #12)